Julie Meyer

THE STORY OF A WAGON TRAIN GIRL

by Dorothy and Thomas Hoobler
in conjunction with Carey-Greenberg Associates
illustrations by Robert Gantt Steele

SILVER BURDETT PRESS
Parsippany, New Jersey

Many women and men kept diaries about their journeys on the Oregon Trail. We have used several of them in writing this story. The most important sources were the journal of Esther Belle McMillan Hanna; the diary of Charlotte Stearns Pengra; the stories of Philura V. Clinkinbeard as retold by her daughter, Anna Dell Clinkinbeard; and the memoirs of Adrietta Applegate Hixon and Jesse A. Applegate.

Dorothy and Thomas Hoobler

Text © 1997 by Carey-Greenberg Associates
Concept and research by Carey-Greenberg Associates
Illustrations © 1997 by Robert Gantt Steele

 Published by Silver Burdett Press
A Division of Simon & Schuster
299 Jefferson Road, Parsippany, New Jersey 07054

Designed by JP Design Associates

Manufactured in the United States of America
ISBN 0-382-39642-1 (LSB) 10 9 8 7 6 5 4 3 2 1
ISBN 0-382-39643-X (PBK) 10 9 8 7 6 5 4 3 2 1

Library of Congress Cataloging-in-Publication Data
Hoobler, Dorothy.
Julie Meyer: The Story of a Wagon Train Girl/by Dorothy and Thomas Hoobler; Carey–Greenberg Associates; illustrated by Robert Gantt Steele.
p. cm. (Her Story)
Summary: Julie and her family join a wagon train traveling from Indiana to Oregon during the 1800's, enduring many challenges while on the difficult five-month journey.
[1. Overland journeys to the Pacific–Fiction. 2. Frontier and pioneer life–Fiction. 3. Family life–Fiction.] I. Hoobler, Thomas.
II. Steele, Robert Gantt,, ill. III. Carey-Greenberg Associates.
IV. Title. V. Series.
PZ7.H76227Ju 1997
[Fic]–dc 20   96-21315 CIP   AC

Photo credits: Photo research: Po-Yee McKenna; 122, top: © CORBIS-BETTMAN, bottom: © Brown Brothers; 123, left: The Oregon Historical Society, ORHI 1645, right: © The Oregon Historical Society, CN 002989; 122-123, © Brown Brothers; 124, © Brown Brothers.

Table of Contents

Chapter 1
We're Going West!

Julie was worried. Poppa had gone off to town again. She knew it had something to do with the farm. The past year had brought the Meyer family a lot of trouble. A tornado had swept across northern Indiana in the spring of 1847. It blew the roof off the Meyers' barn. Fixing that had taken weeks. So they hadn't gotten the crops planted in time.

And wouldn't you know, they had an early winter. As Poppa said, "If it wasn't for bad luck, we'd have no luck at all." The harvest had been so poor that they'd had to sell all but two of their cows because they couldn't feed them over the winter.

On the other hand, Momma always tried to look on the bright side. "We're lucky the tornado didn't hit the house," she kept reminding them.

All that winter Momma still put a hearty dinner on the table every night. She had planted cabbages in the summer, and there were still plenty of them under the snow. Momma and her mother, Nanna Schroeder, knew how to use every part of a chicken too–even the bones. Nanna also showed Julie where to find mushrooms and how to tell which ones were poisonous.

But Julie suspected that something else was wrong. It probably had to do with money. That must be why Poppa went to town so often this winter–to go to the bank to try to borrow money.

Of course, nobody had told Julie anything. Even though she was eleven years old, they thought she was too young to know about some things.

Nanna Schroeder knew what was wrong. She knew everything. But when Julie asked her, she just winked and said, "Might not be here next year." Nanna had been saying that as long as Julie could remember. Nanna usually meant that she might not be here, because she was nearly seventy. (She would never tell just how old she really was.) But this time, Julie thought Nanna might have something else in mind.

Could they lose the farm? That had happened to a family who lived nearby. Julie had been friends with two of their daughters. They had moved down to Cincinnati, where their father hoped to find a job. Julie never heard from them again.

It would be terrible, Julie thought, to have to live in a city. With everybody crowded close together, and all the dirt and noise. She loved being able to go barefoot in the summer, to ride a horse, to see all the plants start to grow each spring. She'd never want to live anyplace but a farm.

Late in the afternoon, when Poppa came riding back from Logansport, he had a big smile on his face. Julie was relieved. She helped him pull off his boots at the door, so the snow wouldn't be tracked inside. Momma was particular about clean floors.

"Is everything all right?" Julie asked.

Poppa smoothed his big red mustache, first one side then the other. He did that whenever he was thinking. "I have a surprise," he said.

She looked at the leather saddlebag he had hung up on the wall. "Not in there," Poppa said. "You'll have to wait. I want to tell everybody all at once. Agnes and Henry are coming for dinner."

Agnes was Julie's older sister. She and Henry Richter had gotten married last June. They hoped to have their own farm one day, but for now Henry worked at a carpenter's shop in Logansport. He and Agnes lived in a boardinghouse, but every Sunday they came to the Meyers' house for dinner. Momma's cooking was a lot better than what was served at the boardinghouse.

"It's not Sunday," Julie said.

"Even so," Poppa replied. "It's a special day for all of us. Agnes and Henry too."

What did that mean? Julie was itching to know.

"Your brothers are playing out in the snow," Poppa said. "Go out and make sure Herman doesn't lose his gloves." Herman was four, but Julie was sure that her other brother, Nick, could watch out for him. Nick was only a year younger than Julie.

She could see, however, that Poppa wanted to get her out of the house so he could tell Momma about the big surprise.

Sighing, she began to lace on her own boots. They were getting tight, because she had grown a lot lately. She hadn't mentioned it because Poppa always complained about how much new boots cost.

She found Herman out by the barn. He was happily sitting in the snow, piling up little mounds of it. Major, the family dog, kept sniffing at the mounds as if they might contain something good to eat.

Herman's coat was unbuttoned, and, as usual, he had lost his gloves. Julie had to hunt around and put them snugly back on his little hands, which were red with the cold.

"Where's Nick?" Julie asked him.

"Nick hunting," Herman told her. He pointed toward the crab apple trees near the barn. Momma had picked them clean that fall, dried the apples, and stored them to use in pies.

Julie walked over there, with Major following. She found Nick crouched behind a fort he had made. He had a pile of snowballs next to him. When he heard Julie coming, he turned and motioned for her to be quiet. She crept up next to him, pulling Major down onto the snow beside her.

"What are you doing?" she whispered.

"I'm hunting squirrels," he said.

"Squirrels?"

"They come after the crab apples."

"Momma picked all the crab apples last fall."

"There's some rotten ones still on the ground," Nick said.

Sure enough, as Julie watched, a squirrel scampered into sight. It looked around and began to dig into the snow. Nick stood up and threw a snowball at it.

Major barked. The snowball missed. The squirrel ran away. Major barked again.

"Have you hit any of them?" Julie asked.

"Not yet," he said. "I'll bet I could if Poppa would let me use his rifle."

"What would you do with a squirrel if you did hit it?" she asked.

"We could eat it," he said.

Julie shook her head. "I wouldn't eat a squirrel," she said.

"You would if you were starving."

"Nick, we're not starving. We have plenty to eat."

"Then why is Poppa going to sell the farm?"

Julie took him by the shoulder and made him turn around to look at her. "How do you know Poppa is selling the farm?" she asked.

"I heard him and Momma talking. They thought I was asleep."

"Why didn't you tell me?"

He shook her hand off and turned away. Just then they heard the sound of a horse's hooves coming up the road. It was Agnes and Henry, in the wagon they borrowed to get back and forth from town.

"Poppa said he had something to tell us," Julie said. "But he was smiling."

"He's going to try to make us feel better about it," Nick said glumly. He threw one last snowball at the side of the barn, and they walked back toward the house.

Momma had roasted three chickens for dinner, instead of the usual two she served on Sundays. This was a good idea, for Henry ate as if he were starving. When Agnes married him and moved to town, Julie had thought there would be one less mouth to feed. Instead, at least on Sundays, there seemed to be at least one more.

After they had finished dessert–crab apple pie–Poppa took a sip of coffee and looked around the table. "I have something important to tell all of you," he said. Julie and Nick exchanged worried glances across the table.

"I've sold the farm," Poppa said, and their faces fell. "And first thing tomorrow we're going to start getting ready to go to Oregon."

Julie almost laughed as she saw Nick's mouth drop open. "Oregon?" he said. His voice squeaked.

Poppa nodded. "Oregon. That's the place. There's more land there than you can imagine. That's where the future of the country lies. We're going West!"

Julie was stunned. She had heard about Oregon in school, but it was so far away! "How are we going to get there?" she asked.

"We've saved enough money to outfit a wagon," Poppa said. "We'll go right across the plains. It'll take us about five months."

"Indians," whispered Nick in awe.

"They won't bother us if we travel in a big group," Poppa said.

Julie looked around the table. "But we'll have to leave Nanna," she said.

"Oh, no," Nanna replied. "You won't get rid of me so easily. When I was your age, I crossed the Atlantic Ocean from Germany on a ship."

Julie knew. Nanna had told the children about the trip many times.

"We're going along too," said Henry. "Oregon will be a great place to raise a family." Agnes nudged him and giggled.

Little Herman suddenly got the idea. He banged his spoon on the table. "We're going West," he shouted. "We're going West."

Chapter 2
Getting Ready

For the next month, there was more work to do than ever before. Poppa brought home the wagon they would use to go West. It was as big as the freight wagons that brought supplies to the stores in Logansport. Julie walked around it, trying to imagine what it would be like to live inside for at least five months. "Why are its wheels so high?" she asked. "It's hard to climb up inside."

"We'll have to cross rivers along the way," Poppa told her. "The wheels will keep the bed of the wagon above the water. And I'll put tar between the boards so that if the water is very deep, the wagon can float."

The next day Poppa attached four wooden hoops to the sides of the wagon. Julie and Agnes began to sew a covering that would fit over the hoops.

Meanwhile, Momma and Nanna were packing food to take on the journey. Smoked bacon, walnuts, dried apples, flour, lard, coffee, salt, and sugar were all stored in bags.

Henry, who was a good carpenter, made chests to fit snugly inside the wagon. Julie and Agnes helped pack their clothing, blankets, towels, tools, soap, dishes, forks, knives, and spoons. Cooking pots and barrels for water were attached to hooks on the sides of the wagon.

Julie was surprised at how much the wagon could hold. Even so, they had to leave a lot behind—almost all their furniture, except some feather mattresses and pillows that would make the ride softer inside the wagon. Momma insisted that they take a cast-iron cooking stove, and Poppa figured how to strap it underneath the wagon.

Nanna looked so sad at having to leave her old rocking chair that they decided to tie it to the back. The only other thing Nanna took, besides her clothes, was a little wooden box. When Julie asked what was inside, Nanna only winked. "My treasures," she said.

They decided to take the two cows, even though they would need to be fed along the way. Momma said the children needed fresh milk on the trail, and she could also make butter from the milk. Poppa and Henry would each ride a horse.

They also crated up some chickens, because their eggs would provide fresh food on the trail. That meant taking bags of dried corn to feed them. But as Henry pointed out, if they ran out of corn they could eat the chickens. Julie was pretty sure Henry hoped they'd run out of corn quickly.

As the day for leaving approached, their neighbors came to say good-bye. The Meyers gave away everything they couldn't carry in the wagon. Julie's best friend, Eleanor Hanks, had always liked the little cradle that Poppa had made for Julie's doll. "You can have it," Julie said. "I can only take the doll, Momma says, and nothing else."

"Every time I look at the cradle," Eleanor said, "I'll think of you."

Julie hugged her. "I know what I'll remember," Julie said. "The times we sneaked off by ourselves to swim in the pond."

Eleanor giggled. "I hope you didn't tell anybody about that," she said. "My ma would have a fit."

"I told Momma," said Julie, "but she didn't mind."

Eleanor rocked the cradle. "I hope you make it," she said. "My dad said ... well, you know ... "

Julie was puzzled. "What did he say?"

"He said he wouldn't take us on that kind of crazy trip." Eleanor looked away. "He thinks you'll all be killed."

For the rest of the day, Julie was bothered by

what Eleanor had said. At dinner she asked Poppa about it.

Poppa smoothed his mustache. "Ever since 1843," he said, "hundreds of families have been crossing the plains to Oregon. I have a map and a guidebook so that we can't get lost."

"We won't be alone," Henry added. "We'll take a riverboat from here to Independence, Missouri. That's where the wagon trains gather. We'll join a group, and there won't be anything to worry about."

That evening, while Julie was helping Agnes sew the wagon cover, Agnes said, "I have something to tell you." Her eyes were twinkling. "I'm in the family way."

Julie's eyes widened. "You're going to have a baby?"

"In July," Agnes said. "And we'll still be on the trail then."

Julie could remember when Momma had given birth to little Herman. "Won't you need a midwife?"

"Momma and Nanna know enough about birthing," said Agnes. "I'm a little afraid, but I wanted you to know. If there was any danger, Henry and I wouldn't go on the trip. So don't worry."

A few days later they finished sewing the cloth cover for the wagon. It took almost an hour to stretch it over the hoops, and Julie was afraid they had made it too small. But at last they got it on. It looked like a big cocoon, she thought. You could tie the ends closed to keep out the rain and dust. To make it waterproof, they had dipped the cloth in linseed oil.

Nick wanted to paint a slogan on the cover. "Oregon or Bust!" he shouted. "That's what people going West put on their wagons."

But Agnes put her foot down. "If we wanted to make a spectacle of ourselves, we would have used calico cloth," she said.

Poppa settled the argument by letting Nick paint the wooden parts of the wagon. He used the red paint that was left over from the barn, and pretty soon even the wagon wheels were red.

"I think that's a lucky color," Momma said approvingly. "All of my four children have red hair, just like their father."

Silently, Julie agreed with Agnes that it looked a bit like a circus wagon. But anyway, the cloth stayed white.

The night before they left, the Meyer family ate their last dinner in the old house. Poppa made a big fire in the stone fireplace, and they popped corn and sang songs. Julie snuggled close to Nanna and remembered all the good times they had together in that house.

"Are you sorry we're leaving?" she asked Nanna.

"I guess so," Nanna replied. "But you shouldn't be. I'm old, so I have a lot to remember. You should think about the exciting things that lie ahead of you. This will be a trip you can tell your grandchildren about."

"First thing after we reach Oregon," said Julie, "I'm going to write Eleanor. Just to tell her what an easy trip it was."

Nanna chuckled. "Don't let anyone fool you. It won't be easy. Nothing worthwhile ever is."

In the morning they carried the feather mattresses out to the wagon and laid them down in the back. Julie climbed up and stretched out. It really was as comfortable as a small room. Momma had strung lines along the hoops and put up hooks so they could hang clothing.

Julie crawled to the front seat to watch Poppa hitch up the two oxen he had bought a few days before. The animals looked so big and strong that Nick had already dubbed them Samson and Goliath. Even so, Julie wondered how they could ever pull the heavily loaded wagon.

One by one, Nanna and Momma and Herman all climbed into the wagon. Nick didn't want to ride inside, but Poppa told him that his shoes would soon wear out if he walked. When Nick got in, Major jumped up and put his paws on the back of the wagon. "He wants to ride too," Julie said.

"He'll get hair all over the mattresses," Agnes protested.

"We won't be traveling fast," said Momma. "Major will be able to keep up."

That was certainly true. The man who sold Poppa the oxen had given him a long black whip to make them move. Poppa didn't want to use it. Julie knew that Poppa never mistreated the farm animals. "We live off their bounty," he had told her, "and we should treat them kindly."

But no matter how loud Poppa and Henry shouted at the oxen, they wouldn't budge. Samson and Goliath stood as peacefully as if they were asleep. Finally Poppa cracked the whip over them. Julie cringed at the sound; it was like a gunshot. But it stirred the oxen. She felt the wagon jolt as they strained forward. Their thick shoulders stretched the chains that held the oxen to the wagon yoke.

Poppa cracked the whip again. Slowly, the wagon began to move. Once it got started, it seemed to roll more easily. The oxen steadily marched forward, and the wagon followed jerkily. Everything tied onto the sides clattered and clanked. The two cows tied to the back mooed softly, and the chickens cackled in their crate.

Julie peered around the side of the wagon for one last look at their home. Good-bye, she thought. But then she remembered what Nanna had said, and turned back to look at the road ahead. That was where the future was.

"It'll take forever to get to Oregon at this rate," Nick muttered.

"Five months," Julie told him. "Today's the first day of April, 1848. We'll be there by September."

"We could walk faster."

"Not for two thousand miles." When Julie said it aloud, she realized for the first time what a long trip it would be. She had never been more than twelve miles from home.

Chapter 3
Heading for Independence

It was only four miles to Logansport, but Nick was right. They really could have walked the distance faster than the oxen. It took two hours to reach the dock at the Wabash River.

From here to Independence, they would be traveling on rivers. Poppa had arranged passage for them on a barge. Getting the wagon into the flat-bottomed barge was tricky. The oxen were nervous about going down the wooden ramp, and Poppa had to use the whip again.

Once everybody was aboard, however, the trip looked easy. The snow was beginning to melt, swelling the river and making the current flow faster. Julie stood close to the side of the boat, watching the water. "How do you like riding in a prairie schooner?" one of the boatmen asked her.

"I thought a schooner had sails," she said. The

barge didn't have sails; the boatmen guided it along with wooden poles.

The man laughed. "I don't mean this old hulk. I meant your wagon. Didn't you know that's what they call them? Prairie schooners?"

She hadn't known. But when she turned and looked at the wagon, she could see how it got that name. When the wind blew into the wagon, it puffed up the white cloth cover. She could imagine the wagon sailing across the plains as smoothly as a ship.

By the end of the day, she wished they could travel the whole way to Oregon by river. It was one of those days when the air seemed to promise spring was coming. People walked or rode on horses along the riverbanks. Some of them waved as the boat went past. As Julie watched, farms and little towns appeared and then were gone again. It was like looking at pictures in a book.

The barge stopped only to take on more cargo along the way. At night, Poppa and Henry slept on the deck, and the rest of them in the wagon. It was a little crowded, but snug and warm. Nanna warned them that they might get seasick, as she had coming across the ocean. But nobody did.

The first night, Julie woke up and wondered for a second where she was. But then she remembered, and relaxed, feeling the current carrying them on.

Four days after they started, they reached the southern tip of Indiana. There, the Wabash flowed into the Ohio River, which was larger and muddier. Julie pointed it out to Nick as the boatmen steered the barge into the main current. "That's the end of Indiana," she said.

He nodded. "We'll never see it again."

That was true, she thought. It was sad to think about. "But we're going to a better place," she said to cheer Nick up. And to cheer herself up too.

The Ohio River was busier than the Wabash. Big paddle wheel steamboats were chugging upstream, smoke pouring out of their stacks. The boatmen on the barge had to be careful to steer out of their wake.

Two days later they came to Cairo, Illinois, where the Ohio met the Mississippi River. It was a tiny town, with little more than a few houses and travelers' inns. The Meyers switched boats, taking a steam barge up the Mississippi. The next day they reached St. Louis, Missouri.

Julie caught her breath when she saw the city. All along the docks, dozens of huge paddle wheelers were tied up. Their high smokestacks looked like a black metal forest. She had never seen so many boats. And the city itself was so large that she couldn't see to the end of it.

The Meyers stood on the wharf with their wagon,

the cows, horses, and all the rest of their belongings. Poppa went looking for a steamboat to take them up the Missouri River. Julie hoped he would find one soon. This was the most crowded and noisy place she'd ever seen. Gangs of dockworkers carrying barrels and crates swarmed around her. She stared at the black men among them. Julie had never seen one before. She realized that they must be slaves.

Families like her own hurried along the wharf, heading for one or another of the paddle wheelers. Julie looked at a board that listed the names of the boats and their destinations: New Orleans, Memphis, Cincinnati, St. Paul…and there was one going to Independence! Its name was the *President Harrison.*

And sure enough, Poppa returned with tickets for that boat. Along with him was a short little man wearing a tweed suit and a beaver fur hat. "This is Mr. Lovejoy," Poppa said. "His family is going to Oregon too."

"Pleased to make your acquaintance," said Mr. Lovejoy. "I'm glad to be of service. Follow me now, and I'll make sure you get settled aboard."

As they moved down the wharf, Mr. Lovejoy said, "You're doing the right thing by getting an early start. We have to leave Independence by the fifteenth of April at the latest."

"Well," Poppa replied, "I don't know. I hoped to

allow time to find a big group that we could travel with. And I understand the grass on the plains doesn't grow till the end of April. We don't want to carry extra feed for the animals. They'll need grass for forage."

"People often make that mistake," said Mr. Lovejoy. "If you travel with a big group, you'll lose time whenever someone else has trouble. People who haven't *planned* properly." His voice showed that he disapproved of people who didn't plan.

"Consider," Mr. Lovejoy went on, "Huge herds of buffalo roam wild on the plains. They have no trouble finding forage in winter. They dig for it in the snow."

Julie had been listening with interest. "I read that the buffalo move from place to place in search of food," she said.

Mr. Lovejoy looked down at her sternly. She felt that he didn't much approve of children who spoke up when they weren't asked.

"If that is true," said Mr. Lovejoy, "what of it?"

Julie really didn't want to answer, but Poppa said, "Mr. Lovejoy asked you a question, Julie."

"I'm sorry," she said. "But you see, the buffalo go wherever they want. Won't we have to stay on the trail?"

Mr. Lovejoy snorted. "That's exactly my point.

The ones who travel earliest will find the best forage."

He turned to Poppa and said, "Your daughter is very bold spirited, I see." Julie knew she had better not say any more.

The *President Harrison* was a double-decker boat with paddle wheels on both sides. Julie had never seen anything like it. It had gingerbread-style railings along the upper deck, where the passenger cabins were. The wagon and livestock were stored on the lower deck, at the waterline. Major wanted to go to the upper deck with them, and they had to tie him to a wagon wheel.

The whole Meyer family stayed in one cabin. The room had no furniture at all, so they carried mattresses up from the wagon to sleep on. Early the next morning, the ship's bells rang and Julie could feel the engine roaring way down below the deck. She heard the splash as the big paddle wheels began to turn.

She dressed herself quickly and went out on the promenade, a walkway that surrounded the upper deck of the boat. From up here she had a wonderful view of the river.

The door of the cabin next to theirs suddenly opened. Julie stepped back as Mr. Lovejoy emerged. He nodded briefly to her and said, "Good morning."

Right after him, through the doorway came a woman and three girls. They too nodded and hurried to keep up with Mr. Lovejoy. They walked in a line, with the mother first and the youngest daughter last. All of them pumped their arms up and down as they walked.

Julie put her hand to her mouth to keep from laughing. The Lovejoys reminded her of a family of ducks. After they passed by, Nick and Herman came outside, and the three of them ran forward to the front rail.

The wind blew against their faces as the boat steamed along. "It must be going at least ten miles an hour," Nick said. They watched as the ship's captain steered out of the way of sandbars and rocks in the river.

Several times the Lovejoy family passed by them in their never-ending walk around the promenade. "After you went out," Nick told Julie, "Poppa told us that Mr. Lovejoy recommended we prepare for the trail by walking around the ship twenty times a day."

Julie groaned. "Are we going to have to do that?"

"I don't think so," Nick said. "Momma and Nanna said it was silly to exercise just for the sake of it. They wanted to rest."

"I can't rest," said Julie. "I'm too excited. But I don't want to walk around in circles all day. Don't tell Poppa I said so, but I hope we don't have to travel with the Lovejoys."

Chapter 4
A Scary Story

When they reached Independence, Julie saw more wagons than she could count. Many other families had arrived before them, getting ready to make the trip across the prairie.

From a distance, all the wagons looked alike. But as the boat drew closer, Nick nudged Julie. "You see?" he said. "Everybody has something painted on their wagon cover."

He was right. When they unloaded their own wagon, she saw that even the Lovejoys' wagon had a slogan on it: *A careful start makes a good end.* Julie smiled. Poppa believed that too.

After they had brought their wagon ashore, Nick begged Poppa to let him write something on it. "At least our family name," said Nick. "Lots of wagons have that. If we got lost, it's the only way we could tell which wagon is ours."

Poppa shrugged and looked at Momma, who sighed. "Agnes and Julie made the wagon cover," Momma said. "Nick has to ask them."

Julie could see that Nick had his heart set on it, so she agreed. But Agnes was stubborn. "It's not the *only* one with nothing on it," she said. She pointed to another wagon nearby, but just as she did, a man started to paint it. "The McNabbs," he wrote, and then he drew a big three-leafed clover in green paint.

Henry laughed. "They're Irish, I guess," he said. "What do you say, Agnes? Let Nick paint something that will bring us luck."

Agnes thought about it. "Do you have any red paint left?" she asked Nick.

He grinned. "I brought the bucket."

"Can you paint a rose?"

Nick frowned. "You mean like a flower?"

"Rose is the name I picked out for our baby," said Agnes. "So you can paint that, if you have to."

Nick grumbled, but he gave in. He had always liked to sketch, and Julie thought the rose he painted looked pretty good. She told him so, and he just snorted and said, "Too bad for this baby if it's a boy."

Poppa and Henry went off to see about joining a wagon train. Julie walked over to the McNabb wagon. One of the McNabbs was a girl about her age, and Julie hoped to make a friend. On the boat, none of the Lovejoy girls would speak to her. She suspected that their father warned them about "boldspirited girls."

"I'm Julie Meyer," she said. "Are you going to Oregon?"

"We are," the other girl replied. "My name's Margaret, but you can call me Peggy."

Julie smiled. "My real name's Julietta."

"Have you heard about the Donner party yet?" Peggy asked.

"No," said Julie. "What's that?"

"It's made everybody worry about the trip West. The Donner family was part of a big wagon train that headed for Oregon two years back. They had terrible troubles along the way. It's much worse out there than people say."

"What happened to them?"

"Hard to tell, for sure. There's all sorts of stories." Peggy shivered. "A lot of them died, I know that. My da told ma maybe we'd better not go. Except we sold everything to buy the wagon, you know."

"We did too," Julie told her.

"So it's practically impossible to go back now. We have to hope for the best. Ma says it's in God's hands."

"I hope we'll travel together," said Julie. She went back to her own wagon and helped Momma set up the cooking stove.

"We'll need firewood," Momma told Julie. "Go find Nick and get him to help you bring some back." She gave her a dime. "That ought to buy enough to use for a couple of days."

Julie had to drag Nick away from a crowd of boys who were playing crack-the-whip. She waited until Nick was on the end of the line. The boys joined hands and ran as fast as they could; then the leader stopped and pulled the whole line around like a whip. The boy on the end usually got thrown off. Nick went sprawling, and Julie pulled him up by his suspenders.

"Momma wants you to help me carry some firewood," she said. When he complained, she said, "I've got a dime; if there's a penny left over, we can buy some candy."

They threaded their way through all the parked wagons into the town. Wooden signs in front of the stores advertised everything you could think of. They stopped at one that said "FIREWOOD." Small bundles of wood were piled up outside.

"How many bundles for five cents?" Nick asked the burly man who stood in front of the store. The man laughed and spat some tobacco juice on the ground. Julie was glad Poppa or Henry didn't use tobacco.

"Costs twenty cents for one bundle," the man said.

"Twenty cents!" Julie cried. "Nobody would charge that in Indiana."

"This ain't Indiana, missy," the man said. "This is the last place you can buy anything for 660 miles. Till Fort Laramie, and you'll find prices are higher there."

"As soon as we get out on the plains," Nick said, "we can just cut our own firewood."

"That's what they all think," said the man.

Julie and Nick went looking for Poppa. On the way Nick said, "I heard a story from some of the boys I was playing with."

"About the Donner party?" Julie asked.

"How'd you know?"

"A girl told me."

"Girls shouldn't know about things like that," Nick said.

"Well, why not, I'd like to know," Julie said angrily. "We're all going West together. If there's any trouble, we'll all share it."

"It'll just scare you," Nick said.

"I heard people died," Julie replied.

"But that won't happen to us. I'm not afraid."

"The Donners got caught in the snow when they were crossing the mountains," Nick said. He was trying to scare her now, Julie noticed.

"That's why we're starting early," Julie said.

"They ran out of food," Nick continued, making his voice low and spooky. "Some of them froze to death. And you know what the others did?"

"I guess they tried to keep going."

"They ate the ones that froze," he announced with a horrible grin.

"That's a lie," she said firmly.

" 'Tis not!" he retorted. "I heard it from Jack Ketchum."

"Some boy," Julie said scornfully. "How would *he* know?"

But the tale of the Donner party spread through the families camped at Independence. It made everybody nervous. Maybe it meant they should start as soon as possible. Julie heard some people saying that the wagon trains that left first would have the easiest time of it. Their animals would eat all the grass and leave nothing for those who followed.

The very next morning, the Lovejoys were gone. They had left all by themselves, without telling anybody.

When Poppa heard, he said, "Lovejoy wants to be the first one on the trail. But I think he's mistaken to travel alone."

Julie was secretly relieved. Even so, she hoped that her family would soon be on the trail as well. Because everything cost so much in Independence, the Meyers were eating the food they had brought with them. But they weren't getting any closer to Oregon.

Even Nanna was getting restless. Every day she sat in her rocking chair next to the wagon, knitting. Sometimes she got up to help Momma with the cooking, but Momma told her to save her strength. "What am I saving it for?" Nanna asked. "What little strength I have, I want to use. I'm not going to be a burden on my family."

Poppa went around the camp, looking for others who had ox-drawn wagons. That way, everybody would travel at the same speed. Some families, like the Lovejoys, used mules, which were faster than the oxen. But mules cost more to buy, and according to Poppa were harder to take care of.

Often Julie visited the McNabbs' wagon to talk with Peggy. The McNabbs had oxen too, and one day Peggy told her, "I heard my da talking to yours. We're going on the trail together."

That was great news. Sure enough, that evening

when the Meyers were eating supper, Poppa said, "We're going to move the wagon tonight."

"Are we leaving?" Nick asked.

"We're going to assemble with the rest of the group," Poppa said. "There are ten other families. We'll be set to leave tomorrow morning."

As soon as supper was over, Poppa and Henry went to get the oxen from the corral. Nick went with them, but Momma asked Julie to fetch a pail of water. "We've got to wash the dishes," Momma said.

"We could just wipe them clean," Julie said.

"That's not a good way to start a long trip," Momma replied. "And we'll wash them every night on the trail too."

Julie smiled. Momma wasn't going to change just because they were going on a two-thousand-mile trip. Things would be just the way they were at home. For some reason, that made Julie feel more secure. If Momma had been on the Donner party, they would probably never have gotten stuck in the snow. Momma wouldn't have let that happen.

Chapter 5
The Prairie

Early the next morning, the wagon train set out across the plains. Eleven white-covered prairie schooners headed west along the Kansas River in a long line. Men on horses or on foot whipped the oxen, urging them forward. All the buckets, boxes, tools, and chests that hung on the sides of the wagons clanked. It sounded like a blacksmith's shop.

Following the train were the cattle that each family had brought. A few riders had been assigned to keep them from straying. Major and some other dogs ran alongside the train, barking joyfully.

So did most of the children. It was impossible for them to stay cooped inside the wagons, especially since the sun was warm. As Julie jumped down from the wagon, Momma called her back. "Here," she said, handing Julie a blue cotton bonnet. "Put this on."

"Momma, it's warm," Julie said.

"You have to protect your skin from the sun," Momma insisted, "or you'll turn as red as an Indian."

Julie slipped the bonnet on, but left the strings untied. She found Peggy McNabb, who also had a new bonnet on her head. They pointed at each other and laughed.

Although the snow had melted, the river was still cold. Even so, Julie saw Nick and his friends wading along the bank with their shoes off.

"See that big boy?" Peggy asked. She pointed to a boy with long arms and legs standing next to Nick. "That's Jack Ketchum," Peggy said. "He's stuck-up."

"What do you mean?" asked Julie.

"He likes to show off and act like he's better than anybody else. His da's the leader of the train. Their wagon is first in the line."

"How did he get to be the leader?"

"Well, he's a big strong fella and the other men just naturally let him be leader. He's the only one wanted to be leader, da says. But you can keep his son away from me, as far as I'm concerned."

Julie looked at Jack Ketchum again. As she did, she saw him trip Nick–on purpose. Nick went sprawling into the cold river. He jumped up with his fists doubled, looking ready to fight. But the other boys were laughing, and Nick decided to laugh too. He was much smaller than Jack.

Julie shook her head. She decided Peggy was right about Jack Ketchum.

The wagon train stopped for lunch when the sun was high in the sky. Julie and Nick went to look for firewood. Major tagged along with them. "I don't much like that Jack Ketchum," Julie said.

"You don't even know him," replied Nick.

"I saw him trip you," she said.

Nick shrugged his shoulders. Julie could see he was embarrassed.

"He was just joking around," he said.

"He's a bully," she said.

Major barked and ran forward. He had spotted an animal. Before Major reached it, the animal ducked into a hole in the ground. Almost at once, three or four other animals poked their heads up from other holes. Major went crazy trying to catch them, but they all ducked down before he got there. "What are those?" Nick asked.

"Prairie dogs, I think," said Julie. "I read about them." The animals had grayish-brown fur and were about the size of cats. Julie and Nick looked around and saw that they were in the middle of a whole town of prairie dogs. They made shrill barking noises.

Julie laughed. "They want us to go away," she said.

"I wonder if they're good to eat?" asked Nick.

"We could trap one."

"I don't think we have time for that," Julie said. "And anyway, if we bring back some firewood, Momma will cook us flapjacks."

When they returned, Momma had the batter ready. Everyone was hungry, and she had to make several batches in her old cast-iron skillet. They spread strawberry preserves over the flapjacks and sat on the ground eating them—except Nanna, who ate hers in the rocking chair.

Even before they finished, however, the lead wagon had started to move again. Jack Ketchum's father rode back along the line of wagons. "Hurry up!" he shouted. "We can't waste all day eating."

Momma insisted on cleaning the dishes again, and Julie saw that Poppa was impatient. Most of the other wagons had already started to move forward. "We'll just have to catch up with them," Momma said.

By the time they got started, the other wagons were far ahead. Poppa and Henry tried to make the oxen go faster, but they only seemed to move at one speed.

It didn't really matter, Julie thought. The plains were so flat that the wagons ahead of them were never out of sight. No matter how far behind the Meyers were, they couldn't get lost.

Nick ran on to try to catch up with the rest of the train. Julie decided she might as well sit in the wagon with Momma, Agnes, Nanna, and little Herman. The three women were sewing gowns for the baby that was on the way. Nanna started to teach Julie how to embroider.

Even though the bed of the wagon was piled with feather mattresses, the ride was bumpy. They seemed to hit every rock in the trail. Everybody inside was thrown to the side whenever one of the wheels passed over a big stone or a hole.

After a few hours, Agnes said, "I can't sit up any longer. My back hurts. It feels like all the bones in it are bouncing against each other." They piled up pillows to make her more comfortable lying down.

By now Herman was restless and crabby, so Julie took him out for a walk. The wind was brisk, but the sun shone brightly enough to keep them warm. Herman wandered off into the newly sprouted grass. Pretty soon, Julie saw, even their own wagon was off in the distance.

"Hurry, Herman," she said. "We've got to catch up with the others."

Playfully, he sat down. Right in the middle of a puddle. She pulled him to his feet and tried to wipe off the mud. His pants were a mess, and Momma would be angry.

She tried to pull him along, but Herman was stubborn when he wanted to be. "Carry me," he pleaded. She managed to pick him up, but he was too heavy, and after a few steps, she couldn't go on.

Finally Henry came riding back looking for them. He put Herman and Julie on his horse and led it back toward the wagon. "You should be more careful," Henry said. "There are rattlesnakes in the grass."

"Rattlesnakes?" Julie shivered.

"That's what people say. Just remember, if you hear them rattle, stand still. Don't move at all, and they'll usually leave you alone."

Julie stayed in the wagon for the rest of the day. As the sun was setting they caught up with the rest of the train. They pitched camp at a spot where there was grass for the cattle.

The work wasn't over. They had to unload the stove again and gather firewood. Julie took Herman's pants to the river to wash them. Nick went to milk the cows at the end of the train. After they ate supper, Momma decided to bake biscuits so they would have something ready to eat in the morning. Julie helped her churn some milk into butter, and afterward wash all the pans and dishes.

Night fell, and the moon shone brightly overhead. Julie was tired, but she heard the sound of music. At the wagon next to theirs, Peggy McNabb's father was playing a lively Irish tune on his fiddle. It attracted a crowd, and a few younger couples started to dance while the others clapped.

Julie walked over to join in the fun. Somebody else showed up with a banjo. All the cares of the day seemed far behind them. By the light of the McNabb's campfire, Julie could see a circle of happy faces.

After about ten minutes, a burly man with dark hair and bushy eyebrows strode into the middle of the circle. He wasn't smiling; in fact, he looked a little angry.

"Well, then!" he said loudly. "I see there's still a lot of energy left in some people. I need volunteers to stand guard over the camp tonight. How about you…you…and you?" He pointed at three of the young men who had been dancing. The music died down. Julie realized this man had to be Mr. Ketchum.

"As for the rest of you," he went on, "we have to get an early start on the trail tomorrow. I'll ring a bell as soon as there's light in the sky. Women who want to cook had better have their fires going by the time the sun's up."

Mr. McNabb made a harsh sound with his fiddle. Some people laughed. It sounded as if he were mocking Mr. Ketchum, who shot him an angry glare.

"All children should be in bed at once," Mr. Ketchum announced. "Don't think you can sleep all day in the wagons. The more weight inside, the slower the oxen will travel. Children who are able should walk."

That ended the fun. Julie felt angry as she went back to her family's wagon. Poppa and Henry were pitching a tent on the ground, where they and Nick would sleep. "Did you vote for Mr. Ketchum to be the leader of the train?" Julie asked Poppa.

He looked at her. "Why do you ask such a question?"

"I think he's a bit of a slave driver," she said. Poppa had often said he opposed slavery. She told him what had happened at the McNabbs' wagon.

"Ketchum was the only one who wanted to be leader," Poppa explained. "And it's better to have someone who's a little harsh than a leader who lets things slide."

Julie bit her tongue. Poppa was probably right. But as she climbed into the back of the wagon, she was still irritated.

She found a place to lie down on the mattresses. It sounded to her as if everybody else was asleep. But as Julie stretched out, Nanna whispered, "Why did they stop the music so soon? It was nice to listen to."

"Mr. Ketchum doesn't like people to enjoy themselves," Julie said.

"Oh, that'll cause trouble later on," said Nanna.

Chapter 6
The Big Blue

For the next two weeks, every day was pretty much the same as the last. Poppa reckoned that the train was making over fifteen miles a day, which was good time.

Sometimes they passed furniture that had been left on the side of the trail. It was clear that some families ahead of them had tried to carry too much. Sofas, chests of drawers, mirrors, and iron stoves were among the discarded objects. A sign on one pile read, "Help Yourself."

But nobody wanted to take anything more in their wagons. In fact, most of the other families in the train started to throw away things too. Especially stoves. They were too much trouble to unload at night and tie up again in the mornings. People just built campfires in a hole and cooked over them.

Momma clung to her own stove long after the

others did. "I can't make biscuits without it," she said. "Or cakes or pies." She knew that Poppa and Henry loved her fresh baked pies. But each day, the Meyers fell behind the rest of the train because they had to wait for Momma's stove to cool before packing it under the wagon.

Around noon of the fifteenth day on the trail, they came to another river—the Big Blue. It met the Kansas River here, and they had to cross over to follow the trail. The Big Blue was a real river, not like the few little streams they had crossed since leaving Independence.

Another wagon sat abandoned on the bank of the Big Blue. One of its wheels was broken, and the cover on top had been partly torn off by the wind. But Julie could read the slogan on it: *A careful start makes a good end.*

"That's the Lovejoys' wagon!" she said. "Poppa, don't you remember? That was what they painted on their wagon."

Poppa nodded. He looked inside. "They left most of what they brought with them," he said. "It looks like they couldn't cross the river."

"But what happened to them?"

Poppa shook his head. "They had mules," he said. "Maybe they rode them across and went on."

"But they'd starve, wouldn't they?"

"They probably took some food. If Lovejoy had a rifle, he might have shot some game. Maybe they could reach Fort Laramie."

"How far is that?"

"Over four hundred miles, I guess. It would have been better for them to turn back. But we didn't see them on the trail."

Julie thought of the three Lovejoy girls. All that practice they had to do to prepare for the trail. Where were they now? What happened to them? She shook her head and tried to think of something Momma would say. "We're lucky we decided to travel in a group," Julie told herself.

That was true. Crossing the river took them most of two days. Mr. Ketchum and Poppa tested the water by riding their horses across. In the middle of the river, the bottom was soft, and the horses had to swim. That meant the wagons would have to be floated across.

Everybody set to work unhitching the oxen and taking the wheels off the wagons. If they kept the wheels on, the wagons would get stuck in the mud.

By the time that was finished, an argument broke out. Mr. Ketchum wanted to start floating the wagons across right away. This time, some of the others opposed him. Julie was glad to see that Poppa was one.

"It'll be dark in an hour, and we can't get every-body across by then," Poppa said. "This is going to be dangerous work, and we can't risk losing some of the animals in the river. We have to wait until daylight."

"That'll mean an extra day lost," said Mr. Ketchum.

"We've made good time so far," Poppa replied. "I think we can spare a day."

Mr. McNabb spoke up in support of Poppa. Several other men agreed. "Our families are at risk too," someone said. "The women and children can't ride in the wagons. They could be swept down-stream."

"How are they to cross the river, then?" asked Mr. Ketchum. "They can't swim."

Julie wanted to say she knew how to swim. But she realized that lots of others couldn't. Agnes wasn't the only woman in the train expecting a baby, and there were also men and women as old as Nanna.

"They can ride the horses across," Poppa said. "We'll have to make several trips."

"That's more dangerous than riding in the wag-ons," Mr. Ketchum argued.

"Let's put it to a vote," said Mr. McNabb.

Mr. Ketchum looked around angrily. He didn't like being challenged. "Well, I'll say this, then," he said. "If you vote for doing it Meyer's way, then I'll step aside. You can choose him to be the leader of the train."

By now, all the women and children had gathered around to listen to the argument. Some of the wives took their husbands aside and began to talk to them quietly.

Mr. Ketchum drew a line on the riverbank with his boot. "Anyone who wants me to continue as leader," he said, "step over here. If you want to follow Meyer, stand there with him."

"That isn't necessary," Poppa said. "We all agreed before that you should be the leader."

"We're voting again now," said Mr. Ketchum. He folded his arms.

Suddenly Mrs. McNabb spoke up loudly. "Don't you think we women should have a say in this too?"

"One vote per wagon," Mr. Ketchum said. "That's the fair way. If your husband lets you wear the pants, that's his affair."

Right away Mr. McNabb walked up and stood next to Poppa. "The McNabb family stands with Meyer," he announced.

Nobody else moved for a moment. They were all uncomfortable with the decision.

Then two men quietly came over and stood next to Poppa and Mr. McNabb. That gave some of the others courage.

In the end, Poppa's side had seven votes; Ketchum's had four. Poppa erased the line in the sand, and stuck out his hand to Mr. Ketchum. "Tomorrow we all stand and work together," Poppa said. Mr. Ketchum nodded and shook hands.

And that was how Poppa became the leader of the train. If Julie had known how much trouble that would cause, she wouldn't have been so happy.

Poppa's first test as leader came that very evening, right after they had finished supper. Momma had baked a crab apple pie to celebrate. Julie was washing the dishes when she heard Poppa talking to Momma.

"Margaretha," he said, "it's time to leave the stove behind."

"Oh, I can't," she said. "I told you, I won't be able to bake."

"We'll keep all your pots and pans," Poppa said softly. "But when we cross the river, the stove will be too heavy. It could cause the wagon to sink. And if that happens…we'll lose everything."

Of course, it would look bad if the new trail leader's wife wouldn't do what he asked. So after thinking a while, Momma said, "At least I have tonight. I'll bake as much as I can to take with us."

For most of the night, Momma and Julie were up baking. Agnes and Nanna helped for a while, but Momma told them both to go to bed. She needed Julie to keep fetching firewood.

Julie had to search pretty far to find the wood. The moon was bright enough to see by, but when she went beyond the edge of camp things got spooky. She began to hear noises. "Just an owl," she told herself, but then jumped when a stick cracked beneath her foot. Did rattlesnakes come out at night?

As she hurried back with her fourth bundle of sticks, a dark cloud covered the moon. Then she heard an eerie howl, and nearly dropped the sticks. "That must be a wolf," she told herself. Even though it sounded far off, she practically ran back.

Momma told her that was enough. "Get some sleep, now," she said to Julie. "I'll finish up soon."

Julie had never been so glad to pull the covers over her. But it seemed she had only a few moments of sleep when Poppa rapped on the wagon. "Hurry up," he said. "We're going first." The Meyers had to lead the train now.

Poppa had planned the crossing carefully. He tied three strong ropes to their wagon. Then he and two other men rode across on horses, tying the ropes to their saddles. Back on the side where the wagon was, Henry and Mr. McNabb tied more ropes to it.

When everything was ready, the horses began to pull. Slowly the wagon inched forward across the bank and into the water. Henry and Mr. McNabb held tight to their ropes, keeping the wagon from washing downriver.

By now everyone in the train was standing on the bank watching. The Meyers' wagon bobbed up and down, just like a boat. It really is a prairie schooner now, Julie thought. The white cover with the rose on it wobbled, and for a second, she thought the wagon would overturn. But Henry and Mr. McNabb were able to steady it. When it reached the other side, everybody cheered.

It took them all morning to bring the rest of the wagons across. It was time to eat lunch, but there was one problem. All their supplies were in the wagons on the far side of the river. But all the people were still on the near side.

Jack Ketchum laughed. "Now we got nothing to eat," Julie heard him say. "Pretty dumb."

Momma stepped forward. She had saved the bread and pies she'd baked all night long. Now she began to pass them out to the others. "These are just going to go stale anyway," Momma said. "This way, we'll all have enough strength to get across after lunch."

Later, Julie asked Momma if she had planned to give out the food all along. "Or did you just do that so Poppa wouldn't look foolish?"

"Your Poppa is never foolish," Momma said. "He had to think about the wagons because he's the leader. The women are supposed to provide the food. I was lucky I had some for everybody."

Julie didn't think luck had anything to do with it.

Chapter 7
Graves on the Trail

A week after they crossed the Big Blue, they saw the first grave. Julie and Nick were walking ahead of their wagon, which was now first in line. The land was so flat here that she could see ahead for miles.

Julie spotted a board sticking up from the ground, and ran ahead to find out what it was. She saw a name written on the board with charcoal: "Evangeline Baxter." And under that, "Went to heaven 7th of May, 1848. Aged 11 years."

When Nick read it, he said, "That wasn't long ago. What's today?"

"The sixteenth of May," Julie said.

"Well, I wonder—"

"Be quiet," Julie said. "This is a grave."

All day long she kept thinking about Evangeline Baxter. The same age as she was.

They passed two more graves on the next day.

And three the day after that. Not all of the dead people were young.

"There's some kind of sickness around here," Nanna told Julie one night. "That's why these people are dying. I hope we get through it quick. I'd like to be buried where there's a tree."

They hadn't seen a tree since they crossed the Big Blue. Besides grass, the only things that grew here were little bushes called sagebrush. Every time the train stopped, the children ran out to gather sagebrush for the cooking fires. But the dried-up little bushes burned so fast that it took a lot of them to keep a fire going.

One day, it began to rain. Rain like they had never seen in Indiana. It poured down so hard that they couldn't see where they were going. The men who drove the oxen were soaked, and everybody else went inside the wagons.

Julie peeked out the back, and saw Major trotting along behind. He looked miserable, but when he saw her he wagged his tail. She knew he wanted to come inside, and he couldn't understand why they wouldn't let him.

They didn't make much progress that day because the wheels of the wagons kept sticking in the mud. After they stopped, it was impossible to build a fire because the rain was still pouring down. "If we'd kept the stove–" Agnes started to say, but Momma hushed her. Like everybody else, they ate cold beans and stale bread for supper.

The rain lasted all night long. Julie could hear it spattering against the wagon cover in the darkness. It made her feel kind of safe, because she was dry. Then there was a loud crack of thunder, and the inside of the wagon lit up for a second. She heard people shouting from the other wagons, but the lightning hadn't hit any of them.

In the morning, the rain finally stopped. Julie and Nick went out barefoot. Momma let them walk without their shoes, because the soles were starting to wear out. The mud felt good, squishing between their toes.

That morning, the prairie sprang into bloom. All around them, thousands of blue and red flowers were opening. The rain had turned the plains into a beautiful garden.

At noon, after the train stopped for lunch, Julie went to pick some of the flowers. When she brought them back, she found Nanna sleeping in her rocking chair. Julie put one of them on Nanna's lap, thinking that she'd be surprised when she woke up.

Momma was trying to start a fire. "Can't you find me some more sagebrush?" she asked Julie. "Everything is too damp to burn."

Julie looked for Nick, but he had gone off some-where with his friends. She whistled for Major, and he was glad to tag along after her.

It was hard to find any dry brush, so Julie wan-dered pretty far from the train. She didn't worry, because it was lovely to walk through the fields of flowers.

Suddenly Major began to bark. Julie looked up. Not far away was a man on a horse, watching her. It took her a second to realize that he was an Indian. He wasn't really red at all, like she had expected. Just kind of very brown, the way you would be if you were out in the sun all day long.

She blushed because he wasn't wearing much except a little cloth around his waist. But he didn't seem to be embarrassed. He said something that she couldn't understand. It must be in his language, she thought.

Major was still barking, and Julie told him to be quiet. The Indian looked over her shoulder, and Julie turned halfway around. He was looking at the wagon train way off behind her. It seemed very far away, and Julie realized nobody would hear her if she called for help.

The Indian pointed at her, and then at the train. Then he waved his hand from side to side. She un-derstood. He wanted them to go away. She nodded,

hoping that he would know she meant yes.

Without speaking again, the Indian turned and rode off. Julie didn't wait around. She ran back to the train as fast as she could. "Momma, Momma!" she shouted. "I saw an Indian!"

Pretty soon, most of the people in the train had gathered to hear her story. Nobody else had seen the Indian, and Jack Ketchum said, "I'll bet she's making it up."

"It's true!" Julie said angrily.

"That's all right, Julie," Poppa said. "We believe you. There's nothing to worry about."

"Why not?" Mr. Ketchum asked. "If there's one, there could be more not far away. They might attack us."

Poppa shook his head. "Back in Independence," he said, "people said the Indians wouldn't attack unless they were threatened. It's their land we're passing through. You'd feel the same way."

"I wouldn't kill anybody for being on my land," Mr. Ketchum said.

"Nobody's been killed," Poppa replied. "If he'd wanted to harm Julie, he could have."

Julie shook her head. "He just wanted us to go away."

"And that's just what we're going to do," said Poppa. "Everybody pack up now. We're leaving."

They didn't see any more Indians in the days that followed. Jack Ketchum made a few jokes about Julie's "friend," but she noticed that Jack didn't stray too far from the wagons whenever they stopped.

Ten days after she saw the Indian on the trail, they saw another wagon train ahead of them. It had stopped, even though it was noon. They couldn't see any cooking fires, either.

As they came closer, a man rode out from the other train on a horse. He was holding a stick with a yellow rag on it. "Stay away!" he shouted at them. "We've got the cholera!"

Cholera! Julie remembered that people were always afraid of cholera, even in Indiana. It was a disease that struck without warning. A person who had it couldn't keep any food down. Then they caught a high fever and became weaker and weaker. Almost everybody who had cholera died. There wasn't any medicine that could cure it.

Poppa led their wagon off the trail to go around the wagon train with cholera. Julie stared at it as they passed by. That must be the train that had left all the graves behind. Evangeline Baxter, aged 11. She had been in that train.

"What causes cholera, Momma?" Julie asked.

"Nobody knows, Julie. Some say it's bad water."

"But wouldn't those people have drunk the same

water we do? From the river?"

"I guess so. Don't think about that."

But when they stopped that night, everyone thought about it. People stopped drinking the river water. They shared the milk from the cows.

"Where's my tea?" Nanna complained.

"We can't drink the water around here," Momma said. "We might get cholera."

"Well, if you put tea in it, it won't hurt me," Nanna said. "Nick, you go fetch some water and put it on to boil."

Nanna calmly drank her tea, sipping it through a sugar cube she held between her teeth. Just as she always did. She put her cup down and noticed everyone watching her. "You needn't wait to see if I'm going to keel over," she said. "I'm more likely to die if I don't get my tea."

In the morning Nanna seemed just as healthy as ever. But a couple of babies had thrown up in some of the other wagons, and everybody worried they had cholera.

Even so, they had to keep going. The day after that, they passed an Indian village. It was far off the trail, but Julie could see the smoke from their fires and the big tents called tepees.

Three Indians on horseback rode up near the wagons and stopped. They carried bows and arrows but didn't shoot any. They just watched.

Mr. Ketchum rode up to the front of the train. He was holding a rifle. "I think I'll scare 'em off," he said.

Poppa moved his horse between Mr. Ketchum and the Indians. "Put that thing down," he said. "The last thing we want to do is start a fight."

"Why not?" Mr. Ketchum asked. "We've got fifteen men with rifles and pistols. They've only got bows and arrows."

"Henry," Poppa said. "Get my rifle from the wagon." It was hanging on a rack inside, and Julie took it down and handed it to Henry.

"Now, Henry," Poppa said. "I'm going to ride over to those Indians, and if Ketchum aims his rifle, I want you to shoot him."

Julie knew Henry had used a rifle only to hunt rabbits, and not very often. Henry looked nervously at Mr. Ketchum, who was glaring at Poppa.

When Poppa started to ride toward the Indians, they took their bows off their backs and strung them with arrows. Julie stood up on the front of the wagon to see, and held her breath.

Poppa raised his hands to show he had no weapon. "We mean you no harm," Poppa said. "We want peace. Peace."

One of the Indians made signs with his hands. He pointed at the wagon train, and then back in the direction they had come from.

Poppa shook his head. He pointed ahead, down the trail. "We go there," he said.

The Indians spoke quietly to one another. Then the leader flapped his hands quickly, like a bird, and pointed the same direction Poppa had.

Poppa nodded and rode back. "They know about the cholera," he told everyone. "They're afraid of us." He looked at Julie. "You were right. They just want us to get off their land quick. They think we're bringing the disease."

Poppa turned to Mr. Ketchum. "Get back to your wagon," he said. "Save your bullets for hunting. We'll see antelope and buffalo before long."

When he left, Henry asked, "Did you really want me to shoot him?"

Poppa pulled on his mustache and smiled. "You don't think I'd keep that rifle in the wagon loaded, do you? That'd be dangerous."

Chapter 8

The Platte

None of the babies who had been sick came down with cholera, but people were still afraid to drink from the river. Whenever it rained, they collected water in buckets.

In a few days the trail turned north, leaving the Big Blue behind. Somewhere up ahead they would reach the Platte River. But now the weather turned hot, and everybody was always thirsty. The cows began to give less milk, and the children were allowed only two cups a day. They had to save most of the water for the animals too.

Every day now the dust rose in clouds from the trail. They all put kerchiefs over their faces, but it didn't help much. Julie's eyes stung and the inside of her nose and throat was scratchy. She wanted to take a drink but a green scum covered the water inside the barrels.

The dust got into the wagons and covered their clothes. Momma fretted terribly because everything was so dirty. Without any water, she couldn't even wash the dishes.

One day when Julie was walking next to the oxen, she heard them snort. Samson and Goliath were usually quiet and gentle. Julie was never afraid to wipe their hooves with grease to keep them from getting sore. Now, suddenly, the two oxen strained at the chains that held them to the wagon yoke.

Poppa noticed it too. "They smell something," he said. For the first time, the oxen tried to gallop. The wagon wheels started to rattle along on the trail. Agnes poked her head out the front. "What's happening?" she said. "We're all being thrown around. Make them slow down."

But Poppa didn't know how. He cracked his whip, but that only made Samson and Goliath go faster. The other wagons followed just as quickly. People from behind started to yell at Poppa, as if he were causing it.

They soon saw what the oxen were headed for. It was water. "It's the Platte River," said Poppa. All the oxen pulled their wagons right up to the river's edge and started to drink. Pretty soon some of the people joined them. "Is it all right to drink, Poppa?" Julie asked.

"I guess so," he said. "It's a different river."

The Platte was the strangest river Julie had ever seen. It was as wide as the Mississippi had been, but it was so shallow that you could walk across. Someone said, "It's a mile wide and an inch deep." In places, there were just little pools, with wet muddy stretches in between.

Momma was annoyed, because the water was useless for washing dishes or clothes. Unless you wanted a mouthful of mud, you had to scoop up a bucket and let it settle for half an hour.

As they traveled along the Platte, they began to see the tracks of animals on the banks. "They aren't horses," Poppa said. "The ones with small hooves could be antelope. And the bigger ones must be buffalo."

Looking for sagebrush that afternoon, Julie found something strange. It was flat and brown and felt like wood, but softer. She tucked it into her basket. When she returned, Momma examined it curiously.

"It looks like it should burn," Momma said. "Good thing, because around here there's hardly anything else to make a fire with."

When she started the fire, the brown thing gave off funny-smelling smoke. "What's that?" called Nanna from her chair. "You've let something fall into the fire."

The smell was bad enough to attract some other people. Mr. McNabb looked at what was burning and turned away. Julie saw that he was laughing. "What is it?" she asked. He just shook his head but went over and told Poppa.

Then Poppa whispered it to Momma, who turned red in the face. Finally she said, "Well, Julie, what this is—is a buffalo chip."

She didn't understand, but Nick did. "That's why it smells," he told her. "This is dried-up buffalo poop."

Julie went right over to the river and washed off her hands.

The next day they caught their first sight of a buffalo herd. It took Julie's breath away. A whole herd of them stood grazing on the prairie as far as she could see. Thousands and thousands of them.

Right away the wagons stopped and the men loaded their rifles. "We're going to have fresh meat tonight!" somebody yelled.

"Hold on," Poppa called. "We ought to get organized." But it looked so easy to shoot a buffalo that everybody wanted to be the first to bring one down. Poppa finally followed the others, telling Henry to stay behind. The Meyers had only one rifle, anyway.

Nanna called Julie to help her stand up. "I want to see," she said. Julie could feel that Nanna was losing weight. She felt lighter than little Herman.

Nanna's blue eyes still sparkled, however, as she gazed off into the distance. "Lots of them, aren't there?" she said.

"Oh, yes, Nanna."

"To tell the truth," Nanna said, "I can't see them so well. But I feel them, don't you?"

It was true. When the men started shooting, the buffalo began to run. The ground started to shake under Julie's feet. It was worse than the time when the tornado roared over their house.

The buffalo made the dust blow up in clouds. Julie couldn't see what was happening. Nanna started to cough. "I need to sit down," she told Julie.

Julie helped her back to the rocking chair. "Are there any trees around here?" Nanna asked.

"None at all, Nanna." Julie thought about that for a second. "Nanna, you can't die. Agnes will need you when she has her baby."

Nanna smiled. "I'd like to see that baby, but it

better come soon." She looked close at Julie. "Don't tell anyone I'm sick, hear? They'll only worry. When you get to be my age, you'll understand. I saw the buffalo, didn't I?"

Julie nodded.

"Well, I would never have seen them in Indiana."

The men were gone for hours. "Of course, that's just like men," Mrs. McNabb said. She and Momma were mending clothes together. "If we wanted to stop and do laundry and air out the mattresses—nothing doing. There'd be all this talk about slowing the train down. But if the men want to run off and shoot at buffalo, then we're just supposed to wait around."

"It would be nice to have fresh meat," said Momma. "I'm tired of bacon. But we're lucky we have it."

Peggy McNabb and Julie were listening. Peggy whispered, "Ma must be worried. She always complains like that when Da does something dangerous."

"Do you think they could get hurt?" Julie asked.

"Well, didn't you feel those buffalo when they ran off? What if they turned around and came back? They'd run right over the whole wagon train."

Sunset came, and the men had still not returned. The women lit the cooking fires as usual, but the camp was very quiet. Even the littlest children stopped playing and shouting.

At last, they heard the sound of hoofbeats and men's voices. Everybody in camp rushed forward to meet them.

And there it was. The buffalo. Only one, but it was so heavy that the men had to tie it to several horses to drag it in.

"Your pa brought it down," Mr. McNabb told Julie.

"Took more than one shot," chimed in Mr. Ketchum. "They're tough beasts, and one man could never have killed it alone."

"Everybody helped," said Poppa.

That night they roasted the buffalo meat on a spit over a big fire. The whole camp gathered around for a taste. It was pretty chewy, Julie thought. It took her five minutes to finish one bite. But for once everybody was happy. Even Mr. Ketchum didn't complain when they stayed up late playing music and singing.

Chapter 9

The Trees at the Bottom of the Hill

Traveling on, they started to see high stone cliffs. At first the cliffs were far off, but they gradually closed in on the trail. Sometimes there was no room for the wagons to get by, and they had to cross the river.

Even though the Platte was shallow, the wagons often got stuck going across. Like everybody else, Julie got behind and helped to push them through the mud.

It was fun at first. The children often sank up to their knees, and their legs made sucking noises as they pulled themselves out. Momma shook her head helplessly when she saw how messy their clothes got.

On one crossing Julie heard a horse start to scream. It was an awful sound, like nothing she had ever heard before. The horse had gotten stuck in a mudhole and was sinking deeper.

"Quicksand," somebody yelled. People looped ropes over the horse's neck and started to pull. But the horse couldn't breathe, and it thrashed around, struggling to get loose. It took a couple of hours before they finally got it out of the quicksand. And then they saw that one of its legs was broken. The man who owned it had to shoot it. There was nothing else to do.

After that, crossing the river didn't seem like fun any more. Every time somebody started to sink into the mud, they remembered the horse.

They began to see dead animals on the trail, mostly cows and horses. Some of them were just bones, picked clean by the buzzards they saw circling in the sky. They made Julie nervous. "How much farther to Fort Laramie?" she asked Poppa one evening.

"I figure it's about 150 miles," he said. "Maybe two weeks more, if nothing slows us down. Tomorrow we should reach a place where the river divides. We'll take the north fork."

He was right, and Julie felt encouraged. But after the crossing, the trail started to go uphill. The oxen huffed and snorted, and their hooves were so sore they needed to be greased every night.

The land around them was rockier than it ever had been before. By now everybody in the train had started to gather buffalo chips for their fires. Nothing else they could find would burn. The smell got into everything, even the mattresses.

One night Julie couldn't stand it any longer. It was like sleeping in a barn. She crept out the back of the wagon. Overhead, the moon shone brightly, and she could see almost as well as in daylight. All the wagons were drawn up in a circle. A couple of men were supposed to be on guard, but they seemed to be sleeping too.

Somewhere off in the distance, a wolf howled. Even though she was used to the sound by now, it made her shiver. She remembered what Eleanor Hanks had said about everybody being killed. Indiana was far away, but they hadn't even come half the way to Oregon yet. It was only June. September seemed a long time off. But there was no way to turn back now.

She sat down and leaned against one of the wagon wheels. She almost screamed when she felt something nudge her back. It was only Major, who usually slept under the wagon. Julie put her arms around him, and soon they were both asleep.

The next day the uphill trail led them out onto a flat plateau. From here, everybody could see mountains off in the distance. They rippled in the air and sometimes disappeared when clouds blew overhead. "Those are the Laramie Mountains," said Poppa.

"We'll reach Fort Laramie at the foot of them."

Each morning it looked like the mountains were just as far away as the day before. Then the wagon train came to the end of the plateau. The trail seemed to end here, and the river ran down a steep hill. Julie stepped to the edge and peered over. Below, she could see dozens of boulders on the slope. Way, way down at the bottom there was a little grove of willow trees.

Julie ached to sit in the shade of a real tree again. But then she thought: How are we ever going to get down there?

It was hard and took them two days. This was the first time they ever had to go down a really big hill. The heavy wagons would run right over the oxen if they went down the regular way. It was going to be like the first time they had crossed a river, only much more difficult.

All the people in the group had to work together to lower each wagon. The Meyers' wagon went first. They tied ropes to it and then pushed it over the side. Everybody took hold of the ropes and held on tight to keep it from going downhill too fast. It was like a tug-of-war. It took half an hour for the wagon to reach the bottom. Henry and Mr. McNabb slid down the hill to untie the ropes so they could be attached to the next wagon.

Poppa said they should let somebody ride in the second wagon. "Most of our people can get down the hill by themselves," he said. "But it's going to be too hard for the older ones and the women expecting babies."

As usual, Mr. Ketchum had a different idea. "We can take everybody down on the horses," he said. "Just the way we crossed the river."

"I don't think anybody should ride a horse down that hill," Poppa argued. "You or me included. We should walk the horses down on foot so they don't stumble."

They were still arguing when Nanna called out from her rocking chair. "Hush, both of you," she said. "I'll go down in the wagon. I'm not afraid."

"No, Nanna," said Momma.

"Why not?" Nanna asked. "Better I should try it than Agnes or one of the other young women. Somebody has to go first. It's either that or stay here, because I'll never be able to walk down that hill."

So they lifted Nanna into the back of the McNabbs' wagon. "I'm fine," she said. "Very comfortable in here. Go right ahead whenever you're ready."

"I'll go with you," Julie said. Before Momma could object, she climbed in next to Nanna.

Slowly the men pushed the wagon to the edge.

Julie held tight to Nanna, who winked at her. Then over the top they went.

The wagon creaked and strained at the ropes as it slowly, slowly descended the hill. Whenever a wheel bumped into a rock, the wagon tipped to the side.

Julie peered out and saw the ropes stretched tight. If they break, she thought, we'll go crashing down to the bottom. She tried to think what Momma would say to make her feel safe.

"I thought this would be more exciting," Nanna said.

"Exciting! Nanna, we could be killed."

"Well, I wish it would go a little faster anyway."

Then the front wheels got stuck on a log. Henry and Mr. McNabb climbed up from the bottom of the hill and tried to drag the log out of the way. It wouldn't budge.

"Give the ropes some slack," Mr. McNabb called to the people on top of the hill.

Julie held her breath as she felt the wagon push harder against the log. Then there was a big BUMP as the wagon rolled over the log. She was thrown back onto the bottom of the wagon.

And then she realized that the wagon wasn't stopping! As it gathered speed, the people on top struggled to hold it back. She heard a loud snap as one of the ropes broke.

The whole wagon turned to one side, and the wheels skidded against the rocks. Julie heard wood cracking, and grabbed hold of Nanna. The wagon is going to turn over, she thought.

But after a few seconds, she heard Nanna's muffled voice. "Let go of me, child. I can't breathe."

Julie realized that the wagon wasn't moving. The other ropes had held. Henry and Mr. McNabb gradually turned the wagon the right way, and someone came down with a new rope.

She took a deep breath. "Nanna, I think I'd rather get out and walk."

"Oh, no," Nanna said. "We're more than halfway down already. That nasty boy–Ketchum's son–he'll tease you if he thinks you were afraid."

"How do you know about him?" Julie asked.

"I hear a lot going on while I'm rocking," Nanna said. "He's just a bully. Stand up to him, and he'll tuck his tail between his legs."

So Julie stayed in the wagon, and it wasn't long before they reached the bottom. "Help me out," Nanna said. "I want to rest under those trees."

The willow grove at the bottom of the hill was even lovelier than it had looked from above. The river widened here into a pool of water that was clear and cool. Julie had the sweetest drink she had tasted in a long time.

Nobody else had what Nanna called an exciting ride. But Momma and the other women rebelled after everybody reached the bottom of the hill. They absolutely refused to go on until they had an extra day to do the washing. The men grumbled about the delay, but not too much. Everybody was exhausted from lowering the wagons.

Not having to travel made it seem like a holiday, even though there was plenty of work to be done. Most of the boys went farther down the river to swim. Momma made Nick take a bar of soap, and told him to wash good and proper. Julie could see by the look on his face that the soap was in no danger of getting wet. Some of the men took the animals off to graze, and others rode out to look for buffalo again.

The women and girls took all the bedding out of the wagons and spread it out in the sun. Everything that could be washed–clothes, blankets, dishes, pots and pans–was given a good scrubbing.

When that was done, the women sat down in a group to mend torn clothing. The girls could do whatever they liked, and Julie and Peggy McNabb went to the river. They waded in the shallows.

"I thought you were about finished yesterday," Peggy said. "When that wagon cut loose, what'd you feel like?"

"I was scared out of my wits," Julie admitted.

"But Nanna didn't even blink an eye. She thought it was exciting."

"Old people are that way," Peggy said. "They've been through so much that nothing can scare them. She sure seemed to like sitting by those trees."

Trees. Julie suddenly remembered what Nanna had said earlier about trees. "I've got to go find her," she said to Peggy.

"What's wrong?" asked Peggy. "She's probably just sitting in her rocker. Ma says she wishes she'd brought one along."

Julie wanted to make sure. She hurried back to their wagon, and was relieved to see Nanna in her usual spot. She was holding her little wooden box on her lap, and had fallen asleep.

When Julie touched her arm, the box slid onto the ground. "Nanna?" Julie said, touching her shoulder. Julie shook her, but Nanna wouldn't wake up.

Julie started to cry, and went to find Momma.

That afternoon, Poppa and Henry dug a grave. It was under the willow trees, where Julie told them Nanna had wanted to be buried.

Momma opened the little wooden box and found letters written in German. "These were from my father," Momma told Julie. "He came to America first, and then wrote Nanna in Germany asking her to come over and be his wife."

There were some other things—a locket with a curl of blond hair in it, and a flower. "That was Nanna's hair," Momma told her. "She sent it to my father with her answer to his letter. But the flower—it's only a few weeks old."

Julie recognized it. It was the one she had left on Nanna's lap when all the flowers bloomed on the prairie. So now, as Poppa read a prayer and some verses from the Bible, she laid it on Nanna's grave.

The next day they had to move on again. It wasn't like home, where you could have a regular funeral and all your neighbors would come over after. Out here, you had to keep moving on and leave the dead behind.

Julie watched the little grove of trees disappear into the distance behind the wagon. It seemed wrong to just leave Nanna there, but there wasn't anything else to do. "Good-bye, Nanna," she whispered. "I promise I'll never forget you."

Chapter 10
Fort Laramie

The trail widened out again, and they could see a long way on either side. Poppa told Julie to watch for some big rocks that were on the map. She thought he was only trying to cheer her up.

A few days later, however, they saw a huge dark mound on the other side of the river. It wasn't a mountain. It was just a big stone all by itself, as if somebody had put it down in the middle of the prairie.

No, that wasn't right. Julie strained her eyes to see. Not far from the big rock was a smaller one. "People call the larger one Courthouse Rock," said Poppa.

"What about the little one?" Julie asked.

"That's Jailhouse Rock."

The name made Julie smile. "How did they get here?"

Poppa shook his head. "God put them here for some reason," he said. Not long after that, an even stranger rock appeared. Sticking up from the flat plain was the tallest thing Julie had ever seen. It rose up like a finger pointing at the sky. They could see it in the distance for two days before they passed by.

"That's called Chimney Rock," Poppa said. "And it means we'll be at Fort Laramie in four days."

Sure enough, just before sunset four days later, the wagon train passed through the wooden gate of the fort. Just inside, Julie saw something even stranger than Chimney Rock. It was the smiling face of Mr. Lovejoy.

He greeted them as if they were his best friends. "Stay close to me," he told Poppa. "There are quite a few swindlers here. I'll show you the best place to get your supplies."

"How did you get here?" Julie asked. "We saw your wagon on the trail."

"An unfortunate mishap," Mr. Lovejoy said. "Nothing could have prevented it. Fortunately another group of travelers passed by and we joined them. I was able to give them the benefit of my knowledge of the trail."

"I thought you'd never been out here before," said Julie.

Mr. Lovejoy looked annoyed, just the way he had

on the riverboat. "Of course I've prepared myself by studying the route on maps."

For some reason, Mr. Lovejoy explained, the other wagon train had gone on without them. Julie had her own ideas why it had left the Lovejoys at Fort Laramie.

"However, I have met an experienced guide here," Mr. Lovejoy told Poppa. "A fur trapper who has traveled the trail many times. If you could find room for me and my family, I could persuade him to travel with us."

Poppa thought this over. "You mean take you with us?"

"And in return, I will persuade my friend to guide the train."

Poppa said he'd have to ask the others. Mr. Lovejoy pointed to the store where they should buy their supplies, and then went off to find the guide.

There were other wagon trains in the fort, along with soldiers, trappers, and some Indians who had come to trade. The center of the fort was like a small town, with stores, a blacksmith's shop, and a saloon. It was a noisy place, even at night.

Ever since Nanna died, Momma had stayed up late working. Now she was unloading a lot of things from the wagon, and Julie offered to help. "No, no," Momma said. "You need your rest."

"Momma, so do you," Julie replied.

"Too much to do tomorrow," Momma said. "I have to figure out what we need to buy."

Julie climbed into the wagon. Herman was already sleeping, but Agnes was awake. "Momma hardly gets any sleep at all," Agnes told Julie. "I wake up and hear her tossing around. She must be thinking about Nanna."

"I miss her," Julie said.

"I do too. I always thought Nanna would be here when the baby came," said Agnes.

"How long will it be?" asked Julie.

"I think about two weeks. People say the first one takes longer."

"Maybe we should stay here till then," Julie said.

"Henry said that too," Agnes said. "But I can't make everybody wait. You can imagine what Mr. Ketchum would say."

"Let the old Ketchums go on without us," said Julie. "We'd be better off."

"No, I'm not going to slow the others down," Agnes said. "Women have always managed to have babies, wherever they were."

Agnes took Julie's hand and put it on her stomach. "I can feel it kick!" Julie exclaimed.

"She's going to be big and healthy," Agnes said.

The store where Mr. Lovejoy told them to go had

outrageous prices. Momma just shook her head when she saw what things cost. But Mr. McNabb came inside before they bought anything. He motioned for the Meyers to follow him.

"I met a shopkeeper from County Mayo, where my parents came from in Ireland," he told them. "He'll sell us what we need at an honest price."

Later that morning, Mr. Lovejoy brought his friend, the fur trapper, to meet Poppa and the others. Julie thought he was the worst-looking man she had ever seen. Or smelled, because if you stood downwind from him you could tell he only took a bath if he fell in a river by accident.

He bragged a lot, though–all about the times he'd fought off Indians and gone over the mountains with no food. "I ate my mules, one by one," he said. "Right through a blizzard so bad that a whole herd of buffalo froze solid. You could walk right up and touch 'em."

Mr. Ketchum was impressed. "You're the kind of man we need to lead us to Oregon," he said.

Julie saw Momma give Poppa a look. Momma's face showed that she felt the same way about the trapper that Julie did.

"The thing is," said Poppa, "I don't see how we'll have room in the train for the Lovejoys. There's five of them."

"Well, you can fit one in your wagon," said Mr. Ketchum. "You've got an extra space now. And I'll take one of them. Who else?"

Julie was angry. An extra space—just as if Nanna had only been taking up room in the wagon.

Nobody spoke up right away. It wouldn't be easy to take a stranger in the crowded wagons.

Mr. Ketchum turned to Mr. McNabb and said, "You ought to be able to fit in one or two more."

Mr. McNabb looked at him. "Tell you the truth, I'm satisfied with Meyer leading the train. We've got by pretty well so far."

"But the trail ahead is much more difficult," Mr. Lovejoy piped up. "We need an experienced person to guide us." He's already talking as if he were part of the wagon train, Julie thought.

Everybody looked at Poppa. He ran his fingers over his mustache. Julie could see he didn't like to decide. "I thank you for your offer," he said finally. "But I think we'd rather go it alone."

Mr. Ketchum's face turned red. "I've put up with this long enough," he told Poppa. "I'm not taking your orders any more." He looked around. "Let's go with this guide, I say. Let the Meyers and the McNabbs find their own way."

But nobody else wanted to break up the train. "We're with you, Meyer," one of the men said to

Poppa. Finally Mr. Ketchum marched off with the guide and Mr. Lovejoy. The rest of the families stayed.

They spent most of the day loading supplies and getting the wagons in shape for the trip ahead. Late in the afternoon, Nick came back to the wagon and crawled inside. That wasn't like him, and Julie went to see what was wrong.

"Go away," he told her. He sounded as if he had been crying. Julie looked closer and saw that he had a bloody lip and a black eye.

"What happened to you?" she asked.

"Nothin'."

"You were in a fight."

"I started it," Nick said. "I gave him a good punch. I'll bet Jack looks worse'n me."

"Jack Ketchum? He's older than you and a lot bigger. Why would you pick a fight with him?"

"He said something I didn't like about Poppa."

Julie got down from the wagon. She felt like the roots of her hair were on fire. Momma always said her hair got redder when she was angry. Well, she was angry now!

She went looking for Jack Ketchum, and soon spotted him in a group of other boys, laughing. His father had started to organize another wagon train, and Jack had new friends.

Julie walked right up to him and gave him a push. "You're a bully," she said. "And you wouldn't dare pick on somebody your own size!"

He was surprised for a second, but then said, "Who's that supposed to be? You?" Suddenly he grabbed her bonnet off her head. Julie's hair fell down around her shoulders.

"Oh, look at all that red hair," Jack taunted her. "Just like your little brothers. I'll bet you're just a bunch of red Indians!"

She rushed at him so quickly that he couldn't get out of her way. She grabbed her bonnet and then clamped it down on his head. "You want it?" she said. "Go ahead and wear it then."

She turned to the other boys, who took a step back from her. "Doesn't he look cute in a bonnet?" she asked. The boys laughed.

Jack was trying to pull the bonnet off, but it stuck tight. "Keep it, then," Julie said. "It looks good on you."

Chapter 11

A Cloud in the Sky

The next morning the Ketchums were gone. They started early with the Lovejoys and a few other families they had met at the fort. "Let them go ahead of us," Poppa said. "I hope we don't see them again."

The Meyers and their wagon train set out the following day. Mr. McNabb's Irish friend had made them take extra barrels of water. "Don't drink from the springs along the trail till you reach Sweetwater River," he said. "The water will make you sick or worse."

Momma wanted to know what happened to Julie's bonnet, but Julie didn't tell her. She wore Agnes's bonnet, because Agnes stayed in the wagon all the time now.

Mr. McNabb's friend was right about the poison springs. They saw dead animals all along the trail. Samson and Goliath were always trying to drink from the water, and Poppa and Henry had to force them back.

In a few days, however, they came to the Sweetwater River. It was clear and good to drink, the best water they'd had in a long time.

They could see high mountain peaks in the distance. "If we follow the Sweetwater," Poppa said, "we'll get to South Pass, which is the only way through the Rockies."

But the trail took them steadily uphill. It was hard now to make even five miles a day. Poppa kept looking for Independence Rock. It was called that because the wagon trains were supposed to pass it around July 4, Independence Day.

On July 4, they still hadn't seen it, but the wagon train celebrated anyway. Momma mixed the last of the crab apple preserves with cinnamon to make a dessert. The men brought back another buffalo and roasted it. Somebody took out a flag and waved it, and Mr. McNabb played a few songs on his fiddle.

But the party didn't last long. People were nervous. They still hadn't passed Independence Rock, and everybody knew the train was behind schedule now.

Two days later Julie saw a dark cloud on the horizon. It didn't look like a rock. "Poppa, I think there's a storm coming," she said.

He looked toward the cloud and tugged at his mustache. "Something else," he muttered. He waved for the wagons to stop, and people gathered around. The dark cloud wasn't high in the sky like an ordinary cloud. It was coming closer fast.

"Tie the cattle and horses to the wagons," Poppa yelled. "Children, get inside."

Julie hardly had time to move before something hit her face. It buzzed, and she reached up to brush it off. It was a big flying insect, as long as her finger. Then the whole cloud of them hit all at once. "Locusts," she heard somebody shout.

By the time she reached the wagon, she was covered with them. They didn't sting, but the noise they made was terrifying. There were so many of them that the sky turned black.

She and Nick plopped into the back of the wagon together. They started to pick the locusts off each other. "Close the cover," Momma shouted. She was holding Herman, who was crying and screaming.

Just then, Agnes cried out. "Momma, I think it's coming!" she said.

For a second Julie thought she meant the locusts were coming. Then Momma pushed Herman into her arms. "Take Nick and Herman and go to the McNabbs' wagon," Momma said. "Tell Mrs. McNabb I need her." Julie understood. The baby! Agnes was going to have her baby.

Julie held tight to Herman's hand as they ran. The flying cloud of locusts smacked against them like hailstones. It was so dark that Julie could hardly see.

She and Nick rapped on the back of the McNabbs' wagon, and Mrs. McNabb poked her head out. "What are you doing outside?" she shouted.

"Momma sent us over here," Julie said. "She needs you to help Agnes."

Mrs. McNabb pulled them up. She opened a chest and got a bottle of something to take with her. "Don't worry, now," she said as she left. "Your sister's going to be just fine."

"What's wrong with Agnes?" Nick asked Julie.

"Don't you know? She's going to have her baby," Julie told him.

"Right now? This is the worst time to pick. Why can't she wait?"

Even though the locusts were banging against the wagon cover, Julie and Peggy giggled.

Julie couldn't tell how long they waited in the wagon. It seemed like hours. The terrible buzzing of the locusts kept on and on. Every now and then, some of them got into the wagon, and they had to catch them to throw them back out. Nick began to crush them in his hands. Julie couldn't bear to do that. But whenever she caught one, she felt its wings rustling inside her fist as it struggled frantically to get loose. Outside, the oxen were bellowing with fear. Poppa and the others had tied the oxen's front feet to keep them from running off with the wagons.

The whole time, Julie kept thinking about Agnes. She wished Momma had let her stay to see the baby get born. Momma probably thought she would be afraid, but she wanted to know what it was like. Even though Agnes had never seemed worried, Julie knew that women sometimes died when they had babies. She shook her head so she wouldn't think about that.

Nanna, she thought, if only you could have stayed with us a few days more. You'd know how to help Agnes.

Finally, the noises began to die down. They could see sunlight through the back of the wagon again. "I'm getting out," Julie said. "I have to find out what's happening to Agnes."

The prairie looked like a desert. Every green thing had been eaten by the locusts. All the grass had been cut off at the ground, and the sagebrushes had lost all their leaves. The locusts had even eaten holes in some of the wagon covers. Some of the horses had broken their ropes and run off. People were walking around, checking the damage.

Julie hurried back to her own wagon. The cover was drawn closed. She didn't remember how long it took to have a baby.

Then she heard it cry, and she scrambled up to look inside. Momma was wrapping the baby in a blanket. "Come in," Mrs. McNabb said. "Take a look at your new little niece."

But the first thing Julie saw was Agnes's face. She looked hot and sweaty, as if she'd been running a long way. Julie stooped down beside her. "Was it bad, Agnes?" she asked.

Agnes licked her lips. Julie could see she had bitten them. But she blinked and whispered, "I heard Nanna. She kept telling me it would be over soon."

Momma put the baby in Agnes's arms. Julie could only see a little bit of her face. It was red and wrinkled. "She really does look like a rose," she said.

Agnes smiled. "I told you," she said.

Chapter 12

Names on the Rock

They reached Independence Rock at noon on the tenth of July. They had seen it ever since the sun rose that morning. It was bigger than any other rock they had seen yet. The whole line of ten wagons was not quite as long as Independence Rock.

The children walked over to look closer. Hundreds of names had been carved on the rock by people who had passed by.

Julie and Nick took sharp stones and added their names, and helped Herman to write his. "We should put everybody's name on," Julie said.

So they wrote Poppa's and Momma's names. "Agnes's and Henry's too," said Nick. "And Rose's." Nick was already proud of telling people he was an uncle.

When they finished, Julie wrote the date. Then she thought for a while. "I'm going to write Nanna's name too," she said. "Even though she didn't really see the rock…I want her name to be here."

Three days later the Sweetwater River ran through a narrow canyon. There was hardly room for the wagons to get by. At the far end of the canyon, two high rocks rose on either side of the trail. As the wagons passed between them, Poppa said, "The map says this is the Devil's Gate."

Julie shivered. "That's such an ugly name."

"It means we're headed for the top of the mountains. The hardest part of the trip is supposed to be ahead of us."

The worst? Julie thought. How could there be anything worse than what they had already gone through?

She soon found out. Every day the trail became steeper. The animals were exhausted after only a few miles.

One of the oxen pulling someone else's wagon died. The man who owned it sat down and cried. His wagon couldn't move with only one ox left to pull it, so the train had to stop.

"You all better go on without us," the man said.

"We're all traveling together," Poppa replied. "We'll take you and your family in our wagons, if we have to."

Henry had an idea. "It'll take half a day, but I

think I can cut his wagon in half. Make it a two-wheeler. One ox can handle that."

Everybody chipped in to help. The family had to leave most of their belongings on the trail, but the two-wheeled cart worked.

The mountains were all around them now. The peaks were higher than any they had seen. We'll never make it over them, Julie thought. But Poppa said that South Pass would take them through.

The weather got colder as the wagons moved higher up. In the mornings, the water in the barrels had ice on it. One day snow began to fall. It was only a few flurries, but it made Julie remember the Donner party. Frozen to death in the snow. But maybe that was only a story. It wasn't even August yet.

But they were still in the mountains when August came. Sometimes the sun warmed everybody up in the daytime, and then when night came they almost froze. Another ox died, and so did some of the horses. The men stopped riding, to save their horses' strength.

All the children had to walk again. They needed to wear shoes because there were always a few inches of snow on the trail now. The soles of Julie's shoes were wearing thin, and her feet got cold.

They came to the end of the Sweetwater River. Springs flowed out of the cliff here. "We've come through the pass," Poppa said. "We're in Oregon now."

Julie was disappointed. She thought the pass would be at the top of a big mountain and then they would go downhill. But the trail still wound upward.

"If we're in Oregon," she said, "doesn't that mean we can stop?"

Poppa shook his head and smiled. "Oregon is huge," he told her. "We've got almost 700 miles yet to travel."

A few days later they met some Indians. Several families of them were camped alongside the trail, and wanted to trade. They had fresh rabbit and buffalo meat. Everybody was tired of eating moldy bacon, so Poppa stopped the train.

People in the wagons brought out things to trade–pots and clothing and furniture. The Indians shook their heads. They pointed to the barrels on the sides of the wagons. They knew they held sugar and flour and coffee.

Julie saw an Indian girl looking shyly at her. She was about the same age. Julie walked over. The girl's hair was braided into pigtails, and she wore a dress made out of a buffalo skin. She smiled and pointed at Julie's dress.

Julie understood that she wanted to feel the cloth, and nodded. The girl rubbed part of the sleeve between her fingers. She shook her head and wrapped her arms around herself. "Cold," Julie said, understanding. "Yes, it's not warm enough for the mountains."

The girl motioned for Julie to follow her. Julie looked back at Poppa, but he was trying to make a trade with the Indian men. She didn't feel afraid, so she followed the girl into the village.

The girl took her to a woman who was stirring a pot over a fire. Whatever she was cooking, it smelled good. The girl pointed to Julie's feet. Julie was embarrassed. By now, the tops of her shoes were flopping loose, and you could see her toes.

The woman went into a tent and brought out a pair of leather Indian boots decorated with pretty stone beads. She put the boots next to Julie's feet. They were the right size. The woman pointed at the boots and then at the wagons.

Julie knew they were offering to trade the boots. But what could she offer for them? She took the girl back to her wagon.

Major growled, and Julie told him to be quiet. The girl pointed at Major. "No," Julie said. "You can't have Major."

Julie climbed into the wagon. The girl stood at the opening in the cover, and peered inside. "Julie!" said Agnes, who was nursing Rose. "What are you doing with that Indian?"

"We're just trading, Agnes. Don't worry," Julie said. She started to rummage through the trunks, looking for something the girl would want. Dresses, towels, underwear–those wouldn't be any good.

"Poppa and the men are doing the trading, Julie," said Agnes.

"I need boots," Julie replied.

"Indian boots?" asked Agnes.

Julie didn't answer. She had thought of something. At first, she couldn't remember where she'd packed it. She had never played with it anyway, because there had been too many other things to do.

At last she found it at the bottom of a trunk. She jumped down from the wagon and showed it to the girl. It was Julie's doll, her favorite–the one she'd picked out to take to Oregon. It seemed babyish to her now. She wouldn't miss it. Agnes had a real baby for Julie to take care of whenever she wanted.

The Indian girl loved the doll though. Julie knew from the way her eyes shone when Julie put it in her arms. They went back to the girl's mother, who frowned. She said something to the girl in Indian language.

The girl spoke back in a soft little voice. She and her mother talked some more. Julie wished she could understand what they were saying.

Finally, the woman threw up her hands. Just the way Momma always did when Julie or Nick talked her into letting them do something she didn't want them to do. The woman handed Julie the boots.

Julie put them on right away. They felt so soft and warm on her feet that she had to smile. The girl's mother laughed and pointed to Julie and then at her daughter. She held up two fingers.

"Yes, we're alike," said Julie. She put out her hand, and the girl took it. "Friends," Julie said.

When Nick saw the boots, he was jealous. But Poppa thought Julie had made a good trade. "The Indians drive a hard bargain," he said. "We offered to trade them a cow, but they wouldn't take it."

Julie thought she knew why. "The cows are losing weight," she said. "Most of them don't give milk any longer."

Poppa nodded. "They're exhausted. It was a mistake to think they could get over the mountains."

The next day the Indians followed them at a distance. That made some people nervous, and Poppa posted extra guards around the camp at night. But the Indians were only waiting for them to reach the Green River.

Julie's heart sank as she saw the river. It was wide and deep. Crossing it was going to be hard, because all the animals were in bad shape. "We can't take the cattle across," Poppa said. "We'll be lucky if we don't lose a wagon or two."

So they turned the cattle loose. Julie thought it was cruel, but Poppa said the cattle would have a better chance of surviving on their own.

And when the wagons had crossed the river, Julie looked back. The Indians were rounding up the cattle. "That's why they followed us," she told Poppa.

He nodded. "They may not live the same way we do," he said, "but they're just as smart as anybody else."

Chapter 13
Fort Hall

After crossing the Green River, the wagon train turned northwest. The Rocky Mountains were behind them now, and the weather wasn't so cold. They began to pass groves of pine trees, so there was plenty of wood for the fires. One day Julie and Nick found wild strawberries growing by the trail and picked two buckets full of them.

"On the map," Poppa said, "there's a fur trading post called Fort Hall about 125 miles away. We should reach it by the end of August."

They saw more graves along the trail now. Two or three every day. Somebody in their own train died—a woman who had two young children. Julie hardly knew her, but she cried when she watched the woman's family lay her into the earth.

They began to travel through the strangest country Julie had seen yet. All around them were black rocks that looked like mounds of bubbles. Henry said that there must have been volcanoes around here a long time ago. The black rocks were made of lava that had cooled.

One day Julie saw two high white mounds, taller than houses. She was curious, and walked over to look. Suddenly she heard a loud whistling sound. She ducked as a spray of warm water poured down on her.

The others heard the noise, and came running. Julie wasn't hurt, just wet. "Is this a volcano?" she asked Henry.

He smiled. "No, it's some kind of odd spring. Look over there." Not far from the white mounds, water bubbled out of the earth. It looked like it was boiling.

Mrs. McNabb bent over and dipped her finger in the water. "'Tisn't hot," she said.

"Don't drink it," Momma warned her. "It could be poisonous."

Mrs. McNabb shook her head. "It's soda water." She gathered some of it in a dipper and showed them the bubbles that rose from the bottom.

"This is a natural soda spring," Mrs. McNabb said. "Let's stop here, and I'll whip up a batch of soda bread."

She was right. You didn't need any yeast to make

bread if you mixed this water with flour. After trying Mrs. McNabb's bread, Momma filled one of their own barrels with the soda water.

Everybody decided it was safe to drink, so Julie tried some. It was too warm, but the fizzy bubbles tickled her throat.

While they were eating lunch, the two white mounds shot water out again. The sound reminded Julie of a steamboat whistle.

"It's caused by the bubbles in the water," Henry said. "They contain gas of some kind. And when the pressure of the gas builds up, the water shoots out of the earth."

Julie wished they could explore longer, but Poppa was eager to reach Fort Hall. "Will that be the end of the trail?" Julie asked.

"No," Poppa said. "There's a long way to go after that."

Julie was tired of hearing that there was still a long way to go. It seemed like years since they left Logansport. Her bones ached, and every night she fell asleep as soon as she climbed into the wagon.

When they finally saw Fort Hall, Julie's heart sank. It wasn't much more than a few buildings made of dried mud. Poppa said it was a trading post for the Hudson's Bay Company. Trappers from all over Oregon brought furs there to sell.

As Poppa was unhitching the oxen, Julie saw a man walk by their wagon. She grabbed Nick's arm. "Isn't that the guide that Mr. Lovejoy wanted Poppa to hire?"

Nick nodded. "I think it is." He looked around. "I don't want to meet up with Jack Ketchum again."

"He looks like he's alone," said Julie. "Let's follow him and see where he goes." Reluctantly, Nick went along. As they got closer, Julie was sure it was the same man. He went into one of the mud buildings. From the sounds inside, they knew it must be a place where liquor was sold.

"I'm not going in there," Nick told Julie.

"Let's wait a minute," she said. "Maybe he'll come out."

As they stood there, they saw all sorts of people walking by. Two men carrying packs of furs wore buckskin trousers, shirts, and moccasins. Both of them had hair longer than Momma's. "They're not talking English," Nick said.

"It must be French," Julie told him." Henry said French trappers from Canada come here."

They saw a man in a long black robe coming toward them. "Is he a minister?" Nick asked.

"I think he's a priest," Julie said. "The French are Catholics, and wherever they go, they take priests with them."

They were a little nervous when the priest stopped to talk with them. They didn't know any Catholics in Indiana. "Were you children with the Lovejoy train?" he asked.

"No," said Julie, "but we know the Lovejoys. Are they here at the fort?"

He shook his head sadly. "I'm sorry to give you bad news. They tried to take a short cut off the trail, but their oxen drank poisoned water and died."

"We thought we saw their guide," Julie said.

"He brought two of the children with him," the priest said. "I offered to let them stay at my mission."

"Is one of them a tall boy with black hair?" Nick asked.

"No, they're both girls," the priest said. "Daughters of the Lovejoys." He hesitated. "Are your parents good friends of the Lovejoy family?"

Julie shook her head.

"From what the guide told me," the priest continued, "the girls may be orphans."

"Orphans? What happened to their parents?" Julie asked.

"Everyone else in the wagon train was too ill to travel," the priest said. "The guide said he had to leave them behind. Has anyone in your wagon train lost a child?"

"You mean did one die?"

The priest nodded. "I've taken in orphans before," he said. "But I have no way to care for them for very long. Families whose children have died on the trail usually are willing to take them."

Julie and Nick looked at each other. "I don't think we have room," Julie said. "But we'll tell our parents what you said."

"They can find me at the mission on the other side of the fort," the priest said.

He walked off, and Nick said, "That was really a terrible guide. How come he didn't know the water was poisoned?"

Just then, the guide came out of the tavern. He looked even worse than when he went in. He walked with a wobble and talked to himself.

Julie forced herself to grab his arm.

The guide jumped as if she'd been a bear. He really wasn't a brave man, Julie thought. "What happened to the Lovejoys and the Ketchums?" she asked him.

"Who're you?" he muttered. "Get away from me."

"I want to know," she insisted. "How could you just go off and leave them?"

He pushed her away. "Those people were the dumbest group I ever seen," he said. "I told them to keep the oxen out of the water, but they didn't listen. No, that big fella, Ketchum, he kept whipping them faster, so they got thirsty."

"But why did the people get sick?" Julie asked.

"Bad meat that they bought at Fort Laramie," he said. "I wouldn't touch it. I tried to bring down a buffalo, but they started firing their guns and scared off the herds. Pilgrims trying to cross the plains! I'm never going to take any again."

Julie and Nick told Poppa and the others what they had heard. As it turned out, the McNabbs were Catholics, and they went to talk to the priest.

So when the train left Fort Hall a week later, the McNabb wagon had two extra passengers.

Peggy McNabb was happier about this than Julie thought she would be. "Da and ma never had any children besides me," she said. "I always wanted sisters to play with. 'Course these two are scared of their own shadows, but I'll teach 'em."

The week of rest had helped the oxen recover their strength. Out of Fort Hall, the trail followed the Snake River. It was well named, for it wound back and forth through a dusty plain.

Once more the people in the train had to tie cloths over their faces. The wind always seemed to come from the west, and each day it blew clouds of dust in their faces.

The Snake River flowed through a narrow gulch, where there was no room for the wagons at all. They traveled on a rocky path high above the gulch. Each day the river seemed farther and farther below them. Whenever they stopped, people had to climb down the cliff to fill their pails of water.

Julie was better at doing this than almost anybody else in the wagon train. Her Indian boots kept her from slipping on the steep cliffsides.

One day the train met another group of Indians. Everybody wanted to trade for a pair of boots like Julie's. Poppa gave their last chicken for a pair. Nobody was more disappointed to see that chicken go than Henry.

It was early September now, and they could feel the chill in the air every night. Every day, Julie thought about the Ketchums and the Lovejoys. She had disliked Jack Ketchum, but never enough to think he might die.

It could still happen to all of us too, she thought. Poppa said there were still more mountains to cross up ahead.

Chapter 14
Riding the Rapids

The wagon train stopped to camp at a waterfall where the Snake River roared down a cliff. Beyond that place, Poppa said, the wagons would have to climb the Blue Mountains. All night long Julie listened to the sound of the falls, praying that they would reach the end of the trail soon.

But there was no easy pass through the Blue Mountains, as there had been over the Rockies. Each day they struggled up the steep slopes. Whenever the oxen had to rest, the drivers chained the wagon wheels together. Otherwise, the wagons would have started to roll back down the mountain.

One night Momma found a swollen tick on Herman's leg. He had picked it up while the children were gathering brush. The next day Herman had a high fever and couldn't walk. Some others in the train caught the fever too. That slowed the journey down even more, for the sick people had to ride in the wagons. Every night Julie checked herself carefully to see if she had any ticks.

It was cold and snowy almost all the time now. Snow made the trail slippery, and the poor oxen struggled to keep on their feet. Momma unpacked winter coats from the trunks. She and Mrs. McNabb used some blankets to make coats for the Lovejoy girls. The girls hardly ever spoke, but they looked so happy when they put on their coats that Julie thought nobody must have ever given them a present before.

Finally, the train reached the top of the mountain, and once more faced the problem of going down the opposite side. This time they locked the wagon wheels with chains so they couldn't roll. The downward slope was so steep that the wagons just slid along.

They headed north, and a cold wind blew against their faces. It was hardly any warmer than it had been in the mountains. When Julie was supposed to be asleep, she could hear the adults talking outside. It was hard to keep secrets in the wagon train.

Everybody was worried about how late in the year it was getting. "If we run into a really bad snowstorm," Mr. McNabb said, "we'll be in trouble." Nobody mentioned the Donners, but Julie knew everyone was thinking about them. That night she dreamed of being smothered in snow.

At the end of September, they reached another river, but their hearts sank when they saw it. It flowed very fast, and looked impossible to cross. Off in the distance was a cone-shaped mountain, and they could see snow covering the peak.

"Are we going to have to go over that mountain?" Julie asked.

"Around it, more likely," said Poppa. "It's Mount Hood, part of the Cascades. If we get through them, we'll be in the Willamette Valley."

"And *that's* the end of the trail?" asked Julie hopefully.

"Yes," Poppa said. "But it will be a hard trip."

Julie didn't need anybody to tell her that.

The wagon train moved along the south bank of the river for several days. Poppa was hoping to find a narrow place where they could ford the river.

They came to an Indian village. Julie saw hundreds of reddish fish hung up on poles over smoky fires. The Indians were taking the fish from the river in nets.

A man walked toward them. Like the Indians, he wore buckskin clothes and tied his hair in braids. But Julie saw that even though his skin was leathery and brown, he had blue eyes.

The man startled everyone when he asked, "Have you got any coffee?"

"You talk English!" Nick said.

The man gave him a smile. "Almost forgot how," he said. "I was born in Virginia, but I've been roaming these mountains since I wasn't much older than you."

He shook hands with Poppa and the others. "My name's Jim Bridger," the man said.

"I've heard of you," Mr. McNabb said.

"Hope it wasn't too bad, what you heard," said Bridger.

"A priest at Fort Hall told me that you knew the mountains better than any man alive."

Bridger laughed. "Well, must be true if a priest said it."

"Can you tell us where we could cross the river?" asked Poppa.

"I sure would like some coffee," Bridger replied. "That's the only good thing all you pilgrims bring with you."

Poppa thought they had no coffee left, but Mrs. McNabb brought out some she'd been saving. "Those fish the Indians are catching," Mrs. McNabb said, "they're salmon, aren't they?"

Bridger nodded.

"Will you trade us some for this coffee?" she asked.

"Well, let's see if we can figure out a trade," Bridger said. "You mind making us some to drink?"

Pretty soon a pot of coffee was bubbling over a fire. Meanwhile, Bridger had walked around the train, looking at the tired oxen and horses. They were so thin that their ribs showed.

"Tell you the truth," Bridger said as he sipped his coffee, "even if you get across the river, those animals won't survive the trail up the mountains. Why not go down the river itself? You'll come straight through to the Willamette Valley."

"How can we do that?" Poppa asked.

"Tear up the wagons and build boats," Bridger said. "Trade your animals for salmon and you'll have something to eat."

Henry thought that was a good idea, but the others were doubtful. "We know the wagons can float," Henry said. "If we take the wheels off, they'll be almost as good as boats."

"The sides aren't high enough," Mr. McNabb told him. "The water will swamp us, and we'll sink."

"We'll tear up a couple of wagons and use the boards to build up the sides of the others," Henry said.

It was a hard decision to make. The wagon train camped overnight so everyone could talk about what should be done.

In the morning they awoke to find the ground covered with snow. That changed people's minds, and they decided to take the river.

Julie was sad when they took off the wagon cover. She remembered how it looked when they put it on. It was dirty now, brown and ragged. The rose that Nick painted had faded.

But the new Rose–Agnes's baby–looked fresh and pretty. Julie was allowed to pick her up and rock her now. "Someday," she told the baby, "I'm going to tell you all about the trip where you were born."

It didn't take more than a few days to build the boats and make some poles from pine trees. Bridger helped them to drag the boats to the bank of the river.

"Farther downstream," Bridger warned them, "you'll see rapids, where the river goes over rocks. Stay close to the bank when you get there. Make sure everyone holds on tight."

As they started off, Julie looked back at Samson and Goliath. She thought they looked as sad as she felt. You carried us such a long way, she thought. I'm sorry we have to leave you behind. But now you can rest at last.

There wasn't any rest for the people in the boats, though. The river carried them along faster than Julie expected. Poppa and the others could barely control the boats with the poles. Everybody else kept busy bailing out the water that splashed over the sides.

The boats rocked back and forth and bounced even more than the wagons had. Poppa had given in when Julie and Nick begged him to let Major go along. But poor Major just lay down in the middle of the boat and whimpered.

Every night they came ashore to camp. The salmon made a tasty meal. Julie and Nick found some berries growing on a tree, and nobody got sick from eating them. We're going to be all right, Julie thought. We're safe now.

During the day, she sat in the front of the boat next to Poppa, hoping that the Willamette Valley would appear. But on either side of the river, all she could see were cliffs and mountains. If anything happened to the boats, she thought—but then she shook her head again. We'll get through, Julie told herself. We've got to!

They passed through some rapids safely, even though the boats bobbed up and down more than usual. But the next day Julie spotted a line of white spray directly ahead. She turned to warn Poppa, but he was already struggling to push the boat toward shore.

The wild motion of the boat excited Herman. He slipped away from Momma, and rushed to look over the side. Julie stood up to grab him.

Just then the boat hit a rock. Julie heard the bottom of the boat scrape and crack. The next moment she caught hold of Herman's coat, and the two of them were thrown into the water.

Herman was screaming. Julie had no time to think about what was happening. She held onto him as tightly as she could. Her legs pumped back and forth, and then she remembered swimming in the pond with Eleanor Hanks. This was different, though. The current carried them downstream like corks.

Julie caught a glimpse of the boat behind them and heard shouts. Then her head went under, and water filled her nose and mouth. Her dress was soaked and heavy, but she kicked out of her boots and managed to swim to the surface again.

Then she felt something pulling her shoulder. She reached back to push it off, and nearly let go of Herman. But then she saw it was Major. He had jumped in after them.

Major helped her to stay afloat, and Julie was able to hold Herman with one arm. She used the other to swim toward shore. She felt one of her feet touch a rock, and she pushed against it hard. They had passed the rapids, and the water didn't flow so fast here.

She saw the shore coming closer, and made one last kick. It took her into the shallows, and she dragged Herman and herself onto the sandy bank.

The next thing she knew, Poppa was carrying her in his arms. Somebody had built a fire. That was good, she thought, because she was shivering.

The sky was dark when she woke up again. That seemed strange to her, and so did the fact that she couldn't move her arms. She realized she was wrapped up in a blanket. When she opened her eyes, Momma was looking down at her.

"It was so lucky you learned to swim," Momma said. Julie laughed. She couldn't wait to tell Eleanor Hanks.

Chapter 15
The End of the Trail

Julie had a problem. Poppa said that the mail boat wouldn't take letters longer than two pages. "How can I tell Eleanor everything about what happened on the trip?" she asked.

"She'll be glad to hear we arrived safely," he said. "Tell her how you saved Herman from drowning."

Everybody thought she was a heroine. Julie was a little embarrassed, because she hadn't really meant to jump into the water. It was an accident. Major was the real hero. And they hadn't all arrived safely.

Every time Julie started to write, she thought about Nanna. Nanna would have loved it here. There were a lot of trees.

The Willamette Valley was so beautiful. Julie understood why people traveled so far to live here. More and more wagon trains were coming in practically every day.

Even so, it would take a long time for the valley to become crowded. It had thousands of acres of good farmland that nobody lived on yet. You could just settle down wherever you pleased.

For a little while they had lived at Fort Vancouver. Poppa and Henry staked out some land and built a cabin large enough for them all. Poppa surprised Momma with a small stove he had bought at the fort. Henry even made a little cradle for Rose. In the spring they planned to build a second cabin.

The McNabbs settled down not far away, and the families often visited each other. Before winter came, the McNabbs told them that Mr. and Mrs. Lovejoy had arrived at Fort Vancouver after all.

"The priest at Fort Hall told them we had their children," Mrs. McNabb said. "They took them off without even a thank you. Acted like we stole them."

"Where did they settle?" Julie asked, hoping it wasn't nearby.

"They went south," Mrs. McNabb said. "To California. They'd heard some wild story about gold being discovered there."

"Did they say what happened to the Ketchums?" Nick asked.

"They pulled through all right too," said Mrs. McNabb. "Too mean to kill, I guess. They headed for California too."

The Meyers had arrived too late to plant a crop, but they had some money left to buy supplies. There were lots of fur trappers at the fort, and they were hungry for home-cooked meals. So Momma bought some flour and began to sell bread. After one of the trappers brought her a bag of cherries, she made pies too.

Poppa didn't much like the idea of Momma working, but she said it wasn't any different from what she already did. They had also saved a bag of yarn, so Julie and Agnes began to knit sweaters and socks to sell to the trappers. And even Nick found a job digging potatoes for a farmer.

One morning Julie woke up to see that snow had fallen heavily during the night. It turned the whole valley into a wonderland. The snow was so deep that she and Nick made tunnels through it.

Poppa went out with his rifle and brought back two wild turkeys. "They can't hide in the snow," he told them. That night the Meyers roasted the turkeys on a spit in the fireplace. Momma had stuffed them with mushrooms that she had gathered.

As Julie was eating her share of the feast, she looked around the room. The firelight flickered over their faces. It was just like home. Nick was teasing Herman by pretending to steal some of his turkey. Agnes and Henry were feeding Rose little bits of bread. Momma asked if anybody wanted more.

Poppa was stretched out with his boots off and his feet toward the fire. Julie reached out and took his hand. "We're not going to move any more, are we, Poppa?" she asked.

"Never again," he told her.

Julie saw Momma smile. "Shall we sing a song?" Momma asked.

Words came into Julie's head, and she began: "Now thank we all our God . . ." As the others joined in, Julie suddenly remembered that this had been one of Nanna's favorite songs.

She stared into the fire and thought, Nanna, you're still with us. You made me think of that song. You stayed with us to the end of the trail.

Timeline

The timeline shows the development of the Oregon Trail, the route that thousands of pioneers used to cross the continent from the Mississippi River to Oregon.

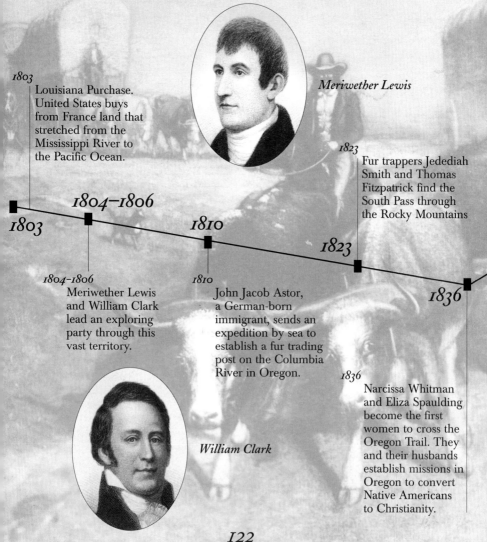

Meriwether Lewis

1803
Louisiana Purchase. United States buys from France land that stretched from the Mississippi River to the Pacific Ocean.

1823
Fur trappers Jedediah Smith and Thomas Fitzpatrick find the South Pass through the Rocky Mountains

1803   *1804–1806*   *1810*   *1823*   *1836*

1804–1806
Meriwether Lewis and William Clark lead an exploring party through this vast territory.

1810
John Jacob Astor, a German-born immigrant, sends an expedition by sea to establish a fur trading post on the Columbia River in Oregon.

1836
Narcissa Whitman and Eliza Spaulding become the first women to cross the Oregon Trail. They and their husbands establish missions in Oregon to convert Native Americans to Christianity.

William Clark

1848
Congress makes Oregon a territory of the United States. It included the present-day states of Oregon and Washington, and parts of Montana and Wyoming.

1843
The "Great Emigration" to Oregon begins. About 1,000 people start out from Independence, Missouri, to cross the plains to Oregon. Thousands more followed in the years between then and the late 1860's.

1859
Oregon becomes a state.

1848

1859

1869

1846–1847

1837   *1843*

1869
Transcontinental railroad completed. People can now travel by train from the Atlantic Ocean to the Pacific Ocean. The era of wagon train pioneers is over.

1846–1847
A wagon train led by George Donner becomes trapped in the snow of the Sierra Nevada Mountains. Thirty-nine of the original 87 members died. Some survivors ate the bodies of the dead to stay alive.

1837
Washington Irving publishes *The Oregon Trail,* which increases public interest in the Far West.

Eliza Spaulding

Narcissa Whitman

123

The True Story

Jim Bridger was a real person. Born in Virginia in 1804, he soon moved with his parents to St. Louis, Missouri. By the time he was eighteen, Bridger had made his first journey to the Rocky Mountains.

Bridger became famous as one of the "Mountain Men"–trappers who roamed the rugged territory between Oregon and the Missouri River. He is said to be the first white person to see the Great Salt Lake. Testing the water and finding it salty, Bridger thought he had become lost and reached the Pacific Ocean.

For decades, Bridger lived among the Native Americans of the region, marrying three women of different tribes. The U.S. government often hired him as a guide for soldiers and exploring parties. In 1843, Bridger built a fort on the Green River in present-day Wyoming. It became a stopping-place for wagon trains on their way to California.

James Bridger